BUTLER AREA PUBLIC LIBRARY
BUTLER, PA.

GIVEN BY

Bucks for Books

Willie, the Frog Prince

Willie, the Frog Prince

C. S. ADLER

1282669

J
F
ADL

CLARION BOOKS • NEW YORK

BUTLER PUBLIC LIBRARY
BUTLER, PENNSYLVANIA 16001

With thanks to Bill Mattsson for sharing.

Clarion Books
a Houghton Mifflin Company imprint
215 Park Avenue South, New York, NY 10003
Text copyright © 1994 by Carole S. Adler

All rights reserved.
For information about permission to reproduce selections
from this book, write to Permissions, Houghton Mifflin Company,
215 Park Avenue South, New York, NY 10003.

Printed in the USA

Library of Congress Cataloging-in-Publication Data

Adler, C. S. (Carole S.)
    Willie, the frog prince / by C. S. Adler.
        p.   cm.
    Summary: In helping his new friend and classmate Marla solve her
problems with her unpleasant home life, eleven-year-old Willie finds
a greater acceptance of and by his perfectionist father.
    ISBN 0-395-65615-X
    [1. Fathers and sons—Fiction.   2. Friendship—Fiction.
3. Schools—Fiction.]   I. Title.
PZ7.A26145Wf   1994
[Fic]—dc20   92-44113
                                                                 CIP
                                                                  AC

AGM   10   9   8   7   6   5   4   3   2   1

For Grayson, my prince of a grandson

Contents

Willie,
the Frog Prince

1

From Under the Desk

*I*t was Dad's first parent-teacher conference. He'd never had the time to come for one before. Willie faced his father and Mrs. Tealso, who were sitting side by side at her desk examining his math and language arts folders. They were discussing him as if he weren't there. He sure wished he wasn't.

"Every one of these work sheets is full of doodles!" Dad said.

"And wild guesses," Mrs. Tealso pointed out with equal disgust.

Willie sank lower in his student desk chair in the front row of the empty fifth-grade classroom. It struck him that his father and Mrs. Tealso were alike. Not in the way they looked. Mrs. Tealso was a ruler-sharp lady with a smooth cap of dark hair and a pursed mouth. Small as she was, she could squelch a whole classroom of rowdy kids with one raised eyebrow. She didn't smile much, and Dad wasn't a smiler either. But Dad was tall, pale, gray haired, and so old that people often asked if he were Willie's grandfather. So then how were they alike?

Dad looked dignified in his gray business suit. He'd worn it, even though he was staying home from work since his disagreement with his boss. "Seeing Mrs. Tealso is important business," Dad had said when Willie had asked him why he was wearing a suit.

". . . Right, Willie?" Dad asked suddenly. His voice echoed in the silent classroom.

"Right what, Dad?" Willie jerked to attention.

"You're going to concentrate from now on," Dad said. His gray eyes nailed Willie. *That* was how Dad and Mrs. Tealso were alike, in the way their eyes pinned him down, Willie realized.

"Right, Dad," Willie said. "Concentrate!" He smiled eagerly. He'd really like to please his father. "Sure, I can do that."

Now four eyes fixed on him doubtfully. Willie's confidence wavered. It was true his mind did have a way of skittering about like a water bug from one interesting thought to another. He could think okay, but not about the same thing for very long. Concentrating might not be that easy.

To Willie's relief, the bell rang for homeroom, and Mrs. Tealso ushered Dad out without further discussion.

Math came first that morning.

While the others were hard at work on their problem sheets in the quiet room, Willie was drawing black ants in a line up Jackson's caramel-colored leg. Each ant had legs and antennas, real as could be. Just as Willie got to the knee, which was as far as Jackson had been able to roll his jeans, Mrs. Tealso caught them.

"What on earth are you up to now, Willie Feldman?"

"It's a surprise for Jackson's sister," Willie said.

"Jackson, roll down your pants leg and get back to work. Willie, show me your problem sheet."

Willie was impressed. Mrs. Tealso sure knew her business. She didn't waste time checking to see if Jackson's work was done. It was, of course, and no doubt correctly. Instead she'd zeroed in on Willie. Caught fair and square, he handed over his scribbled paper. On it was the row of ants that Jackson had admired and asked Willie to reproduce on his leg.

The ants were the only right things on the sheet, Willie suspected. He had always been amazed that anybody's brain could work out how far a car could go in twenty minutes if it was doing forty-eight miles an hour. If it was going sixty miles an hour, he could have figured it out. Sixty was easy. But the driver might get a ticket, especially if he happened to be in a twenty-five-mile-an-hour school zone.

Mrs. Tealso dropped the messy sheet back onto Willie's desk with a sorrowful shake of her head. No ant would find a crumb of anything on her crisp white blouse or narrow skirt. She fairly crackled. "You better finish this for homework," she said. "And what are you whispering to yourself about, Willie?"

"About the problems," he said. "I don't understand them."

That really upset Mrs. Tealso. She prided herself on making kids understand. "Then why didn't you ask me for help at the beginning of the period, Willie? Now there's no time left to explain. Unless," she said hopefully, "you could stay after school?"

The thought of sitting still an additional hour made Willie shudder. Quickly, he said, "No, thanks, Mrs. Tealso. I've got to get home to walk my dog."

"Suit yourself, Willie," Mrs. Tealso said. "I certainly can't help you until you're willing to be helped." She turned her back on him. He felt a little bad about disappointing her again, but very relieved that he didn't have to stay.

That morning language arts followed math. Spelling was a big part of Mrs. Tealso's language arts program. Willie didn't see much sense in spelling. If the *e* at the end was silent, what was it doing there anyway? He decided to add *e*'s to all the words on his list so that he didn't miss any that should have an *e*. It seemed like a pretty sensible idea, but when Nedra, the good speller who was checking his aisle, saw his paper, she burst out laughing.

Willie grinned. He loved to make people laugh, especially girls. He tweaked Nedra's braid. She wasn't a pretty girl. Her teeth stuck out. But her skin and eyes were nice shades of brown like Jackson's, which struck Willie as a funny coincidence. Since Nedra was Indian from Asia and Jackson was African-American, their ancestors had come out brown on different continents.

"Willie!" Mrs. Tealso snapped. "Come up here to my desk."

He went. The teacher leaned back against the desk and frowned at him. "What did you promise your father?"

"To concentrate. . . . I'm trying, Mrs. T."

"Not hard enough. How can I get you to pay attention to your work? I need to put you where there are no distractions." She looked around the room. It was filled with distractions—twenty-eight fifth graders and walls full of posters and bulletin boards and bookcases, not to mention counters with abacuses and plants, and then there were the charts. Mrs. Tealso loved charting things, and Willie could never resist changing ones into sevens or threes into eights or extending the bar a quarter of an inch on any chart he happened to be near.

"I know," Willie said helpfully. "How about under your desk?"

"What? This is no joking matter, Willie."

"No really, Mrs. T. It's the perfect place for me, just like a carrel in the library. Look."

He showed her. If he sat down cross-legged in the knee space under her desk, blank walls surrounded him and the chalkboard wall faced him. Luckily nothing was tacked below the chalkboard, so *that* space couldn't distract him either. "I'll do the spelling list over," he offered.

He could hear the snickers of his classmates, but Mrs. T.'s "Quiet, class" zapped them into silence.

"All right, Willie," Mrs. Tealso said with a sigh of resignation. "But you better behave yourself in there." She handed him his spelling list along with a pencil and a pad to lean on.

This time Willie gave some thought to the word endings. "Believe," he said softly and erased *belive* and spelled it *beleave*. "Siren," he said to himself and erased *sirene* and spelled out *sireen*.

"Receive," he was saying to himself when the door opened and he heard Mrs. Tealso ask what someone wanted. The voice that answered was so soft he couldn't hear, so he stuck his head out of his study hole—far enough out to see a small, plump girl. She had dark, wavy hair cascading to her shoulders like the wild branches of a willow tree. Underneath the hair her face was small, delicate, and scared. She reminded Willie of a kitten he had once saved from a snarling dog that had backed it into a corner.

"New?" Mrs. Tealso said. She made a "tsut" of annoyance. "You'd think they'd give me some warning and not just—oh, well. It's not your fault. Take a seat. There's one left in the back.

"Class," she said, "this is Marla Carter. Who would like to be her buddy to help her get oriented to the school?"

"I would." Willie stuck his hand out of his kneehole space to volunteer.

"Get back to work, Willie," Mrs. Tealso said.

Marla stared at him in wide-eyed wonder, as if she'd never seen a kid under a desk before. Willie smiled to reassure her. She looked so alone there in front of the class.

Nedra was the one Mrs. Tealso picked to be Marla's buddy. Well, Nedra was reliable. She wouldn't be much fun as a buddy, but she wouldn't get Marla lost either. Probably it was good Mrs. Tealso hadn't picked him, Willie told himself. He might get Marla lost. He got lost himself sometimes when he was daydreaming and forgot where he was going.

The bell rang. Willie put his spelling paper on Mrs. Tealso's desk, saying cheerfully, "There you go, Mrs. T. I fixed it for you."

She glanced at the paper and winced. "Oh, Willie!" she said.

"What's wrong?" he asked her.

"You're hopeless. If your father hadn't taken you for those tests, I might think you simply can't do the work. But you do have brains. The problem is you just don't care."

"I care, Mrs. T.!" he cried.

"Not when you can hand in a paper like this. I just don't understand it." She shook her head in dismay.

"Me either. I don't understand it," Willie said. Unless lucky guesses had won him a good score on those learning-potential tests Dad had paid to have him take. That might be it. Because if he really was smart, he wouldn't keep messing up.

The psychologist who tested him had said Willie had a short attention span. "That's no problem," Dad said when Mom reported what the psychologist had told her. "All Willie has to do is concentrate." Dad was really good at concentrating. He could sit all night at his drafting board at home and design the way machines should work together, then get up and go to work the next day and work all weekend if he had to.

Too bad he hadn't inherited Dad's ability, Willie thought. But lately he *was* trying. Why else would he volunteer to sit under Mrs. Tealso's desk?

2

Welcoming the New Girl

Willie always ate his lunch with Jackson at the table next to a window and near the stage in the big cafeteria/auditorium. Usually most of the table was piled high with art projects or parts of backdrops for plays, so he and Jackson had the table to themselves. The only drawback was that Milton and his sidekick, Patrick, sat at the next table, close enough to throw food at them when the cafeteria aide wasn't looking. Milton was the worst tease in the whole fifth grade. Jackson claimed to hate him. To show his loyalty to Jackson, Willie tried to hate Milton, too, but he wasn't a very good hater.

Today Milton was busy blowing straw wrappings at the table full of girls where Nedra was sitting, so Jackson and Willie could eat in peace.

Willie sniffed the delicious-smelling meatballs in the sub Jackson's mother had put in his lunch box.

Then he surveyed the pale, predigested-looking tuna fish dream boat he had bought. "I bet even my dog, Booboo, wouldn't eat this," Willie said.

"You said your dog would eat *any* people food," Jackson reminded him. "And how come you bought it if it didn't look good?"

"For the potato chips," Willie said. "Want some?"

"Okay." Jackson took a few chips.

When he didn't think to offer Willie a bite of his sub in exchange, Willie took his eyes off it and said, "You got the math problems easy, huh?"

"Yeah, they were a cinch," Jackson said.

"Yeah, I thought so." Everything in school was a cinch for Jackson, including sports. The only easy things for Willie were art and making kids laugh.

"I'm sorry you got in trouble about the ants," Jackson said, "but my sister'll freak out when she sees them. Bet she thinks they're real."

Willie doubted that even a five-year-old could be fooled that easily, but he didn't argue.

Suddenly he remembered the new girl, Marla. He peered around the noisy cafeteria and spotted her at the table by the garbage cans that everybody avoided. She was alone. Nedra wasn't being a good buddy. She should have asked Marla to join her table-for-girls-only. It was mean to let someone eat alone on their first day in a new school.

Willie studied his lunch tray. Would she like the

apple or the cookies? He took both, one item in each hand, and whisked himself over to her table.

"Welcome to our school," he said, holding out both hands. "Which do you want?"

She drew back in alarm. "No, thank you," she said.

"It's okay. I'm not trying to trick you or anything."

Her face did a fast-forward of emotions. She caught her lower lip in her teeth. Then, in a sympathetic voice, she asked, "Why did the teacher make you go under her desk?"

"Oh, Mrs. Tealso didn't make me." Willie hastened to defend her. "She's strict, but not mean."

"She wasn't punishing you?"

"No. It was my idea. See, there's nothing under the desk to look at. . . . I get distracted easily," he explained.

"Oh." Another fast play of emotions. "So are you going to sit there all the time?"

"I don't think so," Willie said. "It didn't work too good. I got the spelling test wrong again." He elbowed away the thought of how mad his father would be about that and extended his gifts once more. "So which do you want?"

"You don't have to give me anything," she said.

"But I want to."

"No, thanks," she said. Then she shook her head so hard that her hair swayed like branches in a high wind.

Willie's heart gave a funny skip the way it did when he saw some unexpected flash of beauty, like a rainbow in an oil slick, or a ruby red insect climbing a grass blade.

"I can't be your friend, Willie. Please. I'm sorry," she said.

She knew his name, he thought, and smiled, letting the meaning of her words glance off him. "Here." He thrust the cookies at her because that would be what he'd pick if someone gave him a choice. They were fresh-baked cookies, too, the best part of the lunchroom lunch—which was what he regretted most when he saw the girl toss them in the garbage can on her way out of the cafeteria.

The cookies were like the rest of his day, Willie decided on his way home. All the good stuff had turned out bad—the drawing for Jackson, his idea about working under Mrs. Tealso's desk, even being nice to Marla. He didn't have one good thing to tell Dad he'd done. And Dad would be there at home, waiting for him.

3

Out of Harm's Way

*E*ver since Dad's boss had tried to make him draw up specifications to do a fast fix on a defective boiler because a customer wanted it in a hurry, Dad had been staying home from work. "I won't be responsible if that boiler blows up and kills someone. I don't care if he fires me," Dad had said.

"He won't fire you. You're too valuable," Mom had told him. So far she'd been right. Dad was officially taking some unplanned vacation days, but really he was waiting for his boss to change his mind. Willie admired Dad for doing the right thing and was proud that his father was a man of principle. The only problem was that Dad was keeping himself busy at home by supervising how Willie and Mom and Booboo did things. Actually, he was *criticizing* the way they did things. Going home had been more fun when Dad was away at work and only Mom and Booboo were there to greet Willie.

His spirits rose when he saw his mother in the breezeway. She was shivering even though she was holding the deep collar of her new fur and leather jacket up around her ears. Mom was always cold outdoors in winter no matter what she wore. She said it was because she came from Florida.

"Willie, you better take Booboo for a long walk, a long, long walk," Mom said immediately.

"How come you're out here?"

"To catch you before your father does. He's waiting for you in the kitchen." She pursed her lipsticked lips for the kiss Willie gave her.

"But what'd I do now? I mean, he doesn't know what I did because I didn't get home yet, did I?"

Mom laughed her musical scale laugh. Willie often made her laugh. "It isn't what *you* did; it's Booboo."

"Oh-oh," Willie said. "Booboo's in trouble, too?"

Mom nodded. Then she lifted Willie's chin affectionately and asked, "Did my darling boy do anything really bad?"

He considered. "I don't think so."

"Good. I'm getting tired of battling your father. He gets so worked up over little things that don't matter. What matters is enjoying life, which is something you and I know how to do well."

"I guess." It didn't worry Willie that Mom was criticizing Dad. He knew she loved him. And Dad

loved her. Even though Dad never acted affection-
ate where Willie could see, he did give Mom mushy
birthday and anniversary and Valentine's Day cards
signed, "your loving husband."

Mom's lips twitched. "You know what he told me
today? He said I ought to go out and get a job."

"Are you going to?"

"I might someday. But I won't go back to secre-
tarial work. One boss at home is enough for me."
Dad had been her boss at work before Mom married
him. She had been twenty, and Dad had been a wid-
ower nearly thirty years her senior.

"So what'd Booboo do now?" Willie asked.

"Wet on your father's crossword puzzle."

"Today's puzzle?"

"Right. His fresh *New York Times* crossword puzzle. Booboo just squatted over it and wet."

"He thinks he's still a puppy and paper's okay."

"Never mind what Booboo thinks. He ran and hid
in the yard when your father yelled at him. You'd
better find him and take him for a long, long walk."
Mom took Booboo's accidents lightly. Even when
Booboo had done it on the fluffy white rug in her
bedroom, she'd only screeched for a minute.

"Don't you want to hear about my day first?" Willie really enjoyed sharing what had happened to him
with his mother. No matter what trouble he'd gotten
into, or how badly he'd failed, she was always sympathetic.

"Later. Come back in an hour or so. Your father should be calmer then. *I* won't be. He's driving me crazy with his gloomy classical music, and he says he hates my tapes. Junk music he calls it. As if—"

"Judy!" came Dad's commanding voice.

Willie scrunched into himself even though it was Mom who was being summoned.

"Coming," Mom chirruped. She pushed Willie out of sight around the corner of the house.

Willie opened the gate to their cyclone-fenced backyard. After Willie got Booboo for his tenth birthday last spring, Dad had had the fence put in behind the border of shaggy bushes that screened their yard from the neighbors. Dad liked fences and screens because he valued privacy. Mom didn't care. In the summer she went to her swim club, so she didn't use the yard much anyway.

The lilac bush that Booboo usually favored had already lost its leaves, so smart Booboo was hiding under a leathery-leaved rhododendron. Willie whistled, and Booboo came wriggling out backward. He bounded over and threw his front paws against Willie's chest, nearly knocking him down.

"Want to go for a walk, Booboo?" Willie asked.

For answer Booboo washed Willie's face with his tongue, wagging his tail like a manic windshield wiper. The plumy tail attached to the tall sturdy setter-poodle-Airedale body did look funny, but funny was good from Willie's point of view. Not from Dad's.

He'd frowned at Booboo when Mom and Willie brought him back from the pound.

"*That's* what you picked? I thought you were going to a breeder for a purebred puppy."

"But, Dad, he's playful," Willie had said, "and he loves me already."

"Maybe if we had the tail cut off," Dad had said.

Willie had been horrified. "Booboo's special. He looks like himself," Willie had said. Standing up to his father had never been easy for him, but he'd done it for Booboo's sake, and so far Booboo had kept his tail.

He was waving it proudly as they walked away from their one-story white brick house. Their development was fairly new, with lots of four-bedroom colonial houses with huge lawns, no sidewalks, and plenty of big trees. Willie considered walking over to the next development, where Jackson lived. It was friendlier there. The houses were older, smaller, and closer together. There were street lamps and sidewalks, and more kids out playing. People said hello to you in Jackson's neighborhood. But Jackson was always taking a lesson in something like music or typing. Or he had to go to Boy Scouts, or out with his family.

Instead of checking to see if Jackson was free today, Willie decided he and Booboo would take a long walk alone together. They headed out of the development and crossed the county road to the undeveloped land.

It was mainly fields and woods and dirt roads that dead-ended at isolated old farmhouses and abandoned barns. One particular barn had become Willie's special place because it wasn't locked, and nobody else seemed to use it. Jackson hadn't liked it much when Willie took him there—too dark inside and too many spiderwebs. Jackson's sister wasn't the only one in their family who didn't like crawly things.

Today would be a good day to see how the spiderwebs were doing in the old barn, Willie thought. "How about it, Booboo? Want to walk that far?"

Booboo didn't give an answering bark. He didn't have to. He was always ready and willing. Just the way he pranced along with his poodle-y fur bouncing slightly made Willie feel good.

Booboo stopped to sniff. Willie waited patiently, knowing that was one of Booboo's special pleasures. Chasing things was another, but there were no butterflies or birds to chase in this dead brown and tan winter landscape. Suddenly Booboo looked up. He jerked his leash out of Willie's hand and took off after the airplane zooming by overhead. Booboo's tail flagged his way across the field through the tall dried weeds. No matter. When he ran himself out, he would return.

"And he's a friendly dog, Dad," Willie could say in Booboo's defense when he had to face his father tonight. Cats, chickens, horses, people—Booboo liked everybody. The only person he'd ever bitten was

Dad, and that had been an accident. Dad had stepped on his tail. Also, what could Dad expect when he never said anything nicer to Booboo than "Get out of my chair" or "Stop that, you mutt."

If he kept Booboo away long enough, Willie thought, something might happen to make the crossword puzzle accident seem less important to Dad. And as far as his own performance in school today, it was unlikely Mrs. Tealso would call to report on him when Dad had just seen her this morning. Willie thought about the new girl, Marla. What if she'd moved into that big yellow house with a Sold sign in his neighborhood? What if they had the same bus stop? She didn't seem to like him much yet, but if they spent time together at the bus stop, maybe she would.

Booboo bounded back and jumped up to lick Willie's cheek. "You know what, Booboo?" Willie told him as he hugged the strong woolly body. "Tomorrow I'm going to find out where Marla lives."

4

Someone in the Barn

*T*he roof of the barn was just in sight over the rise of the hill. Willie glanced toward the sagging porch of the lone house in the middle of the empty fields, expecting to see the usual For Sale sign. It had been there for years, and since it meant someone owned the house, Willie had never explored it. His father had drilled respect for private property into him early on.

To Willie's surprise, the For Sale sign was gone and the smoke rising from the chimney meant someone must be living there now. He thought about Marla, but she was too classy to live in that poor a house. Would the people in the house consider the barn theirs, too? But the barn was off by itself, with no signs that it belonged to anybody—mice maybe, and spiders, but nobody human.

Booboo had trotted merrily on toward the barn. Willie hurried after him.

The horse barn hadn't changed. It leaned toward the road, sad-looking despite its faded red paint. But then the whole dead landscape was sad, in drab browns and washed-out yellows. It would take December's first snow to brighten it.

Willie went straight to the latch on the door at the end of the barn without a glance at the two small dirt-encrusted windows on the side. The latch had never had a lock as far as Willie knew. Today it was hanging open. He must have forgotten to close it the last time he was here, he thought. Suddenly a blast of music erupted inside, scaring him and Booboo so they scrambled backward to get away. Booboo began barking hysterically. Willie grabbed him by the collar and dragged him behind the nearest tree, which turned out to be too small to hide them.

When he dared to look again, there, to his delight, was Marla. She was standing in the open doorway, draped in filmy blue stuff like something out of an Arabian Nights fairy tale. "Shush, Booboo," he told his dog, who was now yanking him forward and yipping in eagerness to greet this stranger.

"Don't be scared," Willie advised Marla. "He's friendly."

She offered Booboo a fist to sniff, but he ignored it and stood on his hind legs to lick her face instead. That she resisted. Willie put his arms around Booboo to hold him down and apologized. "He's not that well behaved. But he's glad to see you. So am I. I didn't know you lived here."

She eyed him anxiously. "What are you doing here?"

"Oh, I came by to see what the spiders were up to," he said.

A dimple appeared in her cheek. "You're too much," she said. Then she turned apologetic. "And I hope you're not serious because I cleaned them all out of here."

"You did? Why? Don't you like spiders? They make neat webs. I mean, they come up with really amazing designs. And nothing's prettier than a good web when the sun shines on it after a rain."

"You're a goofball, Willie," she said, and now her face was serious and sad somehow.

"Yeah," he agreed. "But I'm nice anyway. Really, I am."

"Even if you are, I can't be friends with you," Marla said.

"How come?"

"Because you don't fit, and people won't like me if they see me with you. You know how it is."

"Oh," Willie said. He was so hurt he couldn't think of anything else to say. It was because he'd been under the desk when she first saw him, he bet. Boy, that had been a bad idea, one of his worst ever.

"I'm sorry," she said, and she looked as if she really was.

"Well, okay," he said, trying not to show how bad she'd made him feel. "I'll go away, but first, can you tell me how come you're dressed up like that?"

She blushed. "I—it's a costume. I'm practicing a dance."

"No kidding? My mom does dance aerobics but mostly she wears tights. What kind of dancing do you do?"

"I just make up dances about my life. When I grow up, I'm going to have my own dance company."

He nodded, impressed with her ambition. Booboo was nudging his hand now for attention. Willie petted him. "Listen," he said to Marla. "Is it okay if I come here sometimes, I mean, when you're not using the barn? Because Booboo and I like this place. Look, I'll show you. My name's in there."

"What do you mean?" she asked anxiously. "I didn't see any name."

"It's on the post in the middle where the horse stall was. I did it with a jackknife my dad gave me. But then I lost the knife. I came back to look for the knife, and then it got to be a habit."

She took a deep breath and chewed on her lip a while. Then she said, "Okay, if you came here first, then we should share the barn. But let's make a sched-ule—when you can use it and when it's mine." She looked at him nervously, pulling one of her small fingers with the other hand.

"I'm not too good at schedules." Willie grinned at her, hoping she'd relax. He liked that she was trying to be fair.

The music ended and commercials began. Willie saw a book-sized black radio with a silvery antenna on the floor behind Marla.

"Oh, rats," Marla said. "That was the last dance music for an hour. Next comes news."

"So how come you use a radio instead of a tape player?"

"Because I don't own a tape player."

"I could lend you one."

She sighed and rolled her expressive eyes. "No, thanks."

"Why not? I don't use mine much. I'll bring it over tomorrow, and then you can dance whenever you want."

"But I don't have any tapes. And anyway, why should you lend me anything when we're not friends? Please," she said, thrusting the palms of her hands out as if to stop him. "I don't want your tape player."

"Well, okay, then. Bye," he said.

He let go of Booboo and started to leave, but instead of following him, Booboo ran into the barn. "Don't worry. I'll get him," Willie said. He dodged past Marla and went to the wall where the old leather harness pieces hung from nails. Booboo liked to grab the leather ends with his teeth and try to shake them loose from the wall.

Willie saw that the barn had been swept clean. The spiderwebs had been cleaned from the windows. Even the mammoth one between the post and the overhead beam was gone. Marla didn't like spiderwebs any better than she liked him, Willie decided. He untied Booboo's leash from his waist and clipped it onto the dog's collar.

"There," he said to Marla. "Now we'll get out of your way. But if you change your mind about the tape player, let me know. I have a couple of music tapes—a Latin rhythms one my mother gave me when she was trying to teach me to dance, and a *Swan Lake* one my father gave me. It's ballet music. You can dance to that, can't you?"

She didn't answer. Instead, she crouched down and stroked Booboo's head. This time when he tried to lick her face, she just pushed his nose away gently. Booboo got the message. He sat and put one paw on her knee. She rubbed behind his ear. He gave a happy whimper.

"What do you do here besides look for spiderwebs?" Marla asked.

"Oh, sometimes Booboo and I pretend we live here by ourselves. Usually that's when my dad's mad at me. . . . He gets mad at me a lot."

She nodded understandingly.

Encouraged, Willie went on. "I always tell Booboo

it's his job to catch a rabbit or something, but he never does. So then we get hungry and go home. Anyway, Booboo wouldn't kill a rabbit even if he caught one, and me neither. It's just a game—pretending we live here."

"It would be nice to have a tape player," she admitted without meeting his eyes.

Eagerly Willie promised, "I'll bring it tomorrow."

Marla looked mysterious crouching there with the blue veil draped around her. He could see the delicate arch of her nose, and her long, dark eyelashes. Her feelings chased across her face faster than clouds on a windy day. Was she so sad just because she was new? He didn't dare to ask. Too bad Booboo couldn't ask for him. Marla liked Booboo a lot, judging by the way she was still petting him.

"I shouldn't be here anyway," Marla said as if she were talking to herself. "I should be home taking care of Mom. She started getting her headaches again as soon as we got here. She was going to substitute teach—my mother used to be a teacher."

Marla looked up at Willie as if to see if he believed her. "With the headaches Mom can't keep a job, though. They're so bad she can't get out of bed. But I can't take care of her every minute, can I? I need to have some fun sometimes."

"Sure you do," Willie agreed. He firmly believed in fun.

"And how am I ever going to make friends and

fit in anyplace if I'm always—I guess you think I'm selfish."

"No," he said. "I don't."

"My dad says I am." Booboo licked her nose. She giggled. "Silly Booboo. You're cute, but you're silly. You know that?"

Booboo woofed and wriggled at her attention, and she laughed at him. Willie watched enviously. He wished Marla liked silly boys the way she liked silly dogs.

"So where did you live before?" he asked.

"Everyplace." She settled onto the floor and allowed Booboo to prop his head on her leg and fix his eyes adoringly on her face. "My dad doesn't have much luck with his bosses. He's always changing jobs, and usually he wants to try a different place, too."

"I've lived in the same place my whole life. It gets pretty boring."

"Not to me it wouldn't. Do you have any friends?" she asked.

"Just Jackson. When he has the time. He's a good guy, not like some guys in our class. Like Milton. Milton's a tease. You got to watch out for him."

"I had a best friend. I used to go to her dance class with her and watch her, and she let me borrow her tapes to dance with."

"So what happened to her?"

"I told you. We move."

"Yeah. Well, probably you can make friends here easy, and maybe your father will like his job and you'll stay."

"The girls in our class look snobby. That Nedra. She didn't like me."

"Yeah, well, Nedra's sort of picky and—but the other girls are pretty nice."

"When I have my dance company," Marla said, "I'll have lots of friends. Everybody will be my friend, and I'll invite them to pool parties and give them tickets to my shows."

"I'll *buy* a ticket," he said.

"Do you like dancing?"

"Sure," he said, and added hastily, "well, I like to watch."

Booboo had fallen asleep on Marla's lap. Now his feet jerked as if he were running in his dream. They both watched him. "I always wanted to have a dog," Marla said. "You're lucky."

"Yeah," Willie said. For the first time that day he was beginning to feel lucky.

Marla stood up, dumping Booboo, who woke instantly. "I'd better get back. Have fun with the spiders, Willie."

She gave him a smile and picked up the radio. Next thing Willie knew she was gone. He stood there in a daze. Her smile had flashed like magic in the amber dusk of the barn. Next time he saw her, he'd try to make her do it again. Had she told him all that stuff because she'd decided to be his friend after all? He sure hoped so.

"Stop it, Booboo," Willie said when he realized that his dog was barking after Marla. "We can't follow her. She wouldn't like it."

Now what he had to do was remember to bring the tape player tomorrow afternoon, also the tapes. Dad always said, "Willie'd forget his head if it wasn't attached to his neck." And it might be better if Dad didn't know he was lending the tape player. It probably came under the category of expensive things that Dad didn't want Willie lending or giving away, even when they belonged to him.

"Tape player," Willie sang to himself as he and Booboo made their way home. "Tape player, tape player, tape player for Marla."

5

Facing Dad

Going home, Willie noticed the sky was a funny green and lavender. A disk of blinking light passing low over the horizon could have been a plane or a satellite or maybe a spaceship. Willie liked the idea of there being friendly aliens sailing by to check out earth's progress. He waved in case any were watching him.

The walk put him in such a happy mood that he was whistling as he stepped into the kitchen with Booboo, but he stopped in midwhistle when he saw Dad sitting at the table.

"Hi, Dad, what'cha doing?" Willie asked cautiously.

Dad raised his pebbly eyes from his drafting paper and fixed them on Willie. "I'm designing a doghouse," he said. "Where were you?"

"Walking Booboo."

"I didn't see you come home from school."

"I've been walking him since then."

"You might have come in to greet your father first."

"I'm sorry, Dad."

"Do you know that your dog wet on my puzzle?"

"Mom told me. But he didn't mean it. It's just that he thinks paper on the floor—"

"Never mind what he thinks." Dad set his pencil down decisively. "That dog's not a puppy anymore. Since he hasn't learned how to behave, he doesn't belong in the house. He's going to stay in the yard when you're not around."

"Booboo won't like a doghouse, Dad. He likes to be with people."

"When you get him trained, he can be. Meanwhile, you and I will build this doghouse together. It's a project we can share." Dad's smile showed his enthusiasm. He liked projects, especially long, hard ones.

"But, Dad, what if Booboo won't stay in it?"

"He'll learn. You just have to be firm with him and show him who's boss."

"Maybe I could sort of teach him about puzzles," Willie suggested. "I mean, that they're not just regular paper."

"Willie, you've been promising to train that dog since you got him, and you haven't taught him a thing."

"He comes when you call him," Willie argued.

"If he can't do better than that soon, we're sending him back to the pound," Dad said.

"You wouldn't do that to *Booboo,* Dad! He's part of the family."

Dad frowned. "Don't make me out to be an ogre. Booboo's your responsibility, and you've got to learn, too, Willie. What kind of man are you going to grow up to be if you don't know how to behave?"

Willie gulped. Somehow Dad had shifted his criticism from dog to boy, and Willie wasn't sure whom to defend first.

"It's lucky I've got time to devote to your education now, Willie. You need good work habits. Building this doghouse together is an opportunity to start learning some. Tomorrow I'll buy whatever lumber we don't already have in the garage, and we'll go to work the minute you get home from school. How does that sound?"

"I don't know. . . ." Willie began. "I'm not good with tools, Dad. Remember how mad you got when I tried hammering nails in that chair leg I broke?" Willie could remember it well. Dad had yelled so loud it hurt Willie's eardrums.

"Willie," Dad said, and his lips folded in ominously, "I called Mrs. Tealso this afternoon for an update on your behavior. She told me she had allowed you to do your work under her desk. UNDER HER DESK, Willie! She said it was your idea."

"Yeah, Dad, it was." More and more Willie was realizing what a bad idea that had been.

"Did it occur to you that even a normal *five*-year-old would be embarrassed to be seen working under his teacher's desk? I'm sure you knew that, didn't you, Willie. You were just being funny, weren't you?"

"No," Willie gasped. "I mean, yes." What should he say? Either way he was shamed.

"Listen, I don't expect you to come up with straight As," Dad said with hoarse earnestness. "I just want you to stop fooling around and start working. Now is that so much to ask?"

"No, Dad," Willie said. It didn't seem like much the way Dad put it. In fact, it seemed perfectly reasonable. He'd do it. He would stop fooling around, Willie resolved.

Mom stepped into the kitchen, checked something in the oven, and twirled around to say, "Dinner's ready. How about clearing the table, Harold, so that Willie can set it?"

"Come here first," Dad said. "Look at this plan. Isn't this going to be a palace of a doghouse?"

Mom came and fitted her curvy body alongside Dad's lean one. She smoothed back his gray hair and kissed his ear. "It's wonderful, Harold. If Booboo won't use it, it can be a toolshed."

"There you go again." Dad jumped to his feet, shaking her off. "If you backed me up when I try to discipline the boy, he wouldn't be such a mess. It's your fault, Judy, that there's no discipline in this house."

Mom put her hands on her hips and squared off with Dad. "You wouldn't be in such a foul mood if you'd just talk to your boss instead of getting on your high horse and walking out on the job."

"He wanted me to do something that was wrong."

"But if you'd talked, you could have compromised," Mom said.

"There is no compromise with right and wrong," Dad said.

"But, Harold, even world powers negotiate," Mom said.

"WE WERE TALKING ABOUT OUR SON!" Dad yelled.

"I can hear you, Harold," Mom chimed. "The whole world can hear you. You don't have to yell."

"IT'S YOUR FAULT FOR SPOILING HIM!" Dad shot at her.

Mom looked at Willie, who was frozen in place. He was overwhelmed by his parents' fight and filled with guilt that it was over him—as usual.

"Willie, go wash up for dinner. It's late. I'll set the table for you," Mom said. "Go, sweetheart." She gave him a melting smile of encouragement.

Booboo was lying on Willie's bed with his head on the pillow when Willie passed his own room on the way to the bathroom. Instead of washing up, Willie threw his arms around Booboo. Maybe it hadn't been a good idea to go under the desk, but the doghouse Dad had thought up was no better. Booboo would never get used to it. He'd hate it no matter how big and beautiful it was.

"So what's going to happen, Booboo?"

Booboo whined softly and licked Willie's nose.

If he were a better son, Mom wouldn't get yelled at and have to fight with Dad, Willie told himself. Then he thought how Dad looked so old when his face sealed up tight with anger. "You're wearing your grandpa out," the stranger in the airport had scolded Willie when he'd gotten lost and Dad had had to chase around to find him. He was aging his father, wearing him out. And Dad was a good guy. He was brave and honest and smart. He worked hard, and he tried to give his family everything they wanted.

Like the time Willie got lost at the airport. That had been when Dad was taking them to Hawaii to make up for being out of town so many weekends on business. Now how many kids got to go to Hawaii? Jackson's father smacked him sometimes, but Dad never hurt Willie—at least not physically. And if he were a better son, Dad probably wouldn't yell at him so much either. Maybe.

Willie let go of Booboo and went to wash his hands for dinner.

"Concentrate," he reminded himself. "Concentrate and make Booboo behave. Oh, yeah, and make Marla laugh." That was three things he had to do. Three was a lot. And the trouble was, remembering wasn't easy for him. Still, he'd do it. For Dad's sake, he'd do it. He wouldn't let his mind wander. He'd concentrate, concentrate, concentrate. He really would. Tomorrow.

6

Two Puddles for Breakfast

*I*t still shocked Willie to see Dad in slippers at the breakfast table on a weekday. He had always left for work before Willie came downstairs. But Mom, decked out in pink and orange Day-Glo aerobics workout tights and top, was her normal self. The outfit meant that she was in a hurry to leave, and that used to mean they'd have jelly doughnuts for breakfast, Willie's favorite. But with Dad sitting there, Willie could forget the jelly doughnuts. Dad didn't approve of them.

"You certainly don't give yourself much time to make the school bus," Dad said. "Where's your dog?"

"He's sleeping in, Dad. Booboo's not an early riser."

"Neither, it appears, are you," Dad said. "What kind of breakfast can you eat in five minutes?"

"Cereal," Mom supplied before Willie could admit to anything. "You'll have cereal, won't you, Willie love?"

"Okay," Willie said.

Mom leapt to the closet, landing on one foot with the other bent gracefully backward. She leapt back to the table, landing on the other foot. She always leapt around the kitchen before aerobics as a kind of warm-up. "There you are," she sang out and pirouetted to get the milk from the refrigerator.

"Can't he get his own cereal?" Dad asked.

"You get the juice, angel boy," Mom said.

Willie got the juice while she filled a small bowl with cereal and milk for him.

Dad picked up the box after she set it down. He said, "The sugar content in this cereal's too high for Willie. You know the doctor said sugar's bad for him. No wonder he ends up under the teacher's desk. Can't you cook him a proper breakfast, Judy? Oatmeal and toast and scrambled eggs, that's what he needs."

"He's not going to lift bricks, Harold."

"Mental exercise uses up calories, too—which is why I eat an egg and an English muffin before going to work."

As Mom was agreeing that Dad always did eat sensibly, Willie looked up from pouring his juice and saw through the kitchen window that his bus was rounding the corner. Looking down, he saw he'd poured a puddle that was dripping onto the floor.

Dad noticed, of course. Dad noticed everything. "Willie, you klutz! Now look what you've done."

"I've gotta go," Willie said.

"Not before you eat your breakfast."

"Then I'll miss the bus." Booboo ambled into the kitchen, wagged a greeting to everyone, and barked to be let out. Willie moved to open the door for him.

"Hold it right there!" Dad said. He probably thought Willie meant to leave, too. "You sit down and eat your cereal. After you mop up the juice. QUIET, BOOBOO!"

Booboo yipped pathetically as if asking what *he'd* done wrong. Mom slipped over to the door. "The dog has to go out, Harold," she said. "Unless you want him to do his business on the floor?"

As if on command, Booboo squatted and made a second puddle. "I *thought* he got up pretty early for him," Willie said. "I guess he had to go."

Willie's bus driver waited for him a few seconds and then took off.

"I missed my bus," Willie said. He got the squeegee mop out to clean up both accidents. Dad was holding his head. "Do you have a headache, Dad?" Willie asked.

"It's your own fault, Harold," Mom said. "Just remember, it's your fault, not Willie's or Booboo's. Bye, now. I'm off to aerobics." She broad jumped the puddle and disappeared toward the coat closet. But she ducked her head back in to say, "And don't make poor Willie nervous when you drive him to school. He would have made the bus if you'd let him eat his cereal."

Dad opened his mouth to reply, but too late; she'd gone. "I guess I'd better get dressed so I can get you to school, Willie," Dad muttered.

Once he had the kitchen to himself, Willie relaxed. He finished with the mop, rinsed it in the sink, then fed Booboo and put him into the fenced-in yard.

"Don't worry," he told Booboo. "Mom'll let you back in when she gets home. But it might be a while. You know how she is. After aerobics she'll do hospital volunteer stuff or shopping or something. You can run around to keep warm, okay?"

Booboo gave him a loving lick on the chin, and Willie hugged him. It was hard to shut the door on his dog and listen to the pleading yips that began the instant Booboo realized he was stuck in the yard alone.

Next Willie dumped the cereal in the sink and washed down its traces. For breakfast, he took two large chocolate chip cookies from the cookie jar. At the sound of Dad's footsteps, Willie stuck the cookies in his pocket. He was finally drinking his juice when Dad reentered the kitchen.

In the car, Dad said solemnly, "Willie, you should understand that I'm doing this because I want you to be a success in life."

"Driving me to school, Dad?"

"No, giving you standards to follow."

Dad must mean that he shouldn't go under the teacher's desk again, Willie figured. And concentrate. And what were the other things he had to remember? "Don't worry, Dad," Willie said agreeably, "I'm going to shape up. You'll see."

7

One Cookie for Lunch

In homeroom Willie remembered the chocolate chip cookies. One was still uncrumbled. He slipped it onto Marla's desk as he passed. She was hidden under waves of hair, but when she turned, her face appeared and with it a little smile for him.

"She your girlfriend?" Jackson leaned across the aisle to ask him. Jackson never missed anything Willie did. Maybe because his father was a policeman, Jackson took obedience seriously, which meant the nearest he got to fooling around was watching Willie do it. Sometimes Willie deliberately did things just to give Jackson a laugh.

"Willie." Jackson prodded him with a finger. "I asked you. She your girlfriend?"

"I don't think so," Willie said. "She doesn't like me much yet."

"Figures," Jackson said.

"It does? Why?"

"You're not tough enough. Girls like tough dudes."

"I'm tough." Willie clenched his fists and tried to flex his muscles, forgetting that he didn't have any yet.

"Milton's tough." Jackson gestured at Milton, who was showing off to an admiring circle the ink tattoo of a death's head he'd pricked into the skin on the back of his hand. "You're not."

"Girls don't like Milton."

"When he gets older they probably will. Milton's just like my brother, and girls fall all over him."

Willie knew Jackson's brother from the gas station where he pumped gas and checked Mom's oil last summer. In the cutout shirts he wore, Jackson's brother's muscled arms and shoulders certainly were awesome.

"Willie," Mrs. Tealso's voice brought him to attention, "you didn't hand in your permission slip."

"What permission slip?"

"To visit the recycling center this morning." She waited. Willie's mind was a blank on the slip. He must have been thinking about something else when she told them about it. Well, that had been yesterday, before his promise to Dad.

"If you forgot it, I'm afraid you'll have to sit in the office while your class is gone," Mrs. Tealso said.

Willie thought fast. "Could I ask Mrs. Foster if she needs help in the library instead?"

Mrs. Tealso pursed her lips, considering. "All right," she said finally. "And take Marla with you. Unfortunately, she doesn't have a permission slip either."

"Did you give her one to take home?" Willie asked.

Mrs. Tealso raised her eyebrows at him, but when he didn't back down, she came up with a quick excuse. "When someone begins in the middle of the term, there's always confusion."

What that meant, Willie figured, was Mrs. Tealso had forgotten to give Marla a slip.

• • •

"Want me to tell you about the recycling center?" he asked Marla on the way to the library. "I went with my Boy Scout troop last year."

"No, thanks," she said. ". . . You're a Boy Scout?"

"Well, I was until I got kicked out."

"What did you get kicked out for?"

"I kept getting lost."

"Huh?"

"You know, on hikes. We went on all these hikes, and I kept going in the wrong direction or getting left behind or—" He shrugged. "You said I was a goofup, Marla. So you know."

She nodded. "Well, try not to get us lost on the way to the library."

"No problem. . . . So how's your mother?"

She bit her lip, and her face flew storm warnings. "I shouldn't be here," she said in a flurry of words. "Dad wanted me to stay home and take care of Mom. She's got one of her migraines. But I said I had to get to school because in the last school I missed so many days they nearly left me back. And I'm a *good* student. And now here I am wasting the morning. I wish I had stayed home with Mom. At least then I wouldn't feel so guilty."

"Couldn't your dad stay home sometimes?"

"He has to earn a living for us."

"Well, you could hire someone to take care of her."

"That takes money. Dad mostly gets jobs in stores that don't pay all that well. Once he got made store manager, but then they went out of business. He says he's just not lucky."

"Gee," Willie said with sympathy.

Marla's hair hid her face again. Was she crying? Willie felt so sorry for her that he reached out to comfort her. But he jerked his hand back in case she wouldn't like him to touch her.

About all he could do to help was make her laugh, he decided. They were passing the computer room. He ducked in and plucked an endless ribbon of paper with holes in it from the wastebasket. "Here's a necklace for you, Marla," he said, tossing it around her neck, "because you're so beau-ti-ful."

"Stop that, you loon!"

She ripped off the chain, and it fell to the floor just as they reached the library. Mrs. Foster was standing in the doorway of the sunny, blue-carpeted room, which was lined with bookshelves.

"Willie, you're littering the halls," she scolded.

"We were coming to help you," he said. "Please." He fell to his knees. "Don't *you* be mad at me, Mrs. Foster." She laughed. He could make her laugh easily. That was why she was one of his friends in school.

"I'd be glad to have some help shelving books," Mrs. Foster said. "But isn't your class going on a field trip this morning?"

"Yeah, but we can't go. I forgot my permission slip and Marla's new, so she didn't get one."

Mrs. Foster smiled at Marla and told her, "Willie's specialty is forgetting things, but he means well. Last year he brought in twenty-nine overdue books from under his bed. It turned out four of them didn't even belong to the library." Her tinkling laugh ended in a cute little hiccup that made Willie laugh with her.

Marla was studying Mrs. Foster from under her hair as if she didn't know whether to trust the librarian's good humor. Marla didn't trust anybody much, Willie guessed. He'd have to be patient about making her laugh. Maybe paper chains weren't funny. He could write her a poem. Except he couldn't rhyme very well. He could draw her a picture. That was it—one of a girl hiding behind her hair and smiling. He was good at cartoons. But when he saw the return cart overflowing with books, he realized they'd be too busy for him to draw anything.

"Good thing we can be here all morning. You really need us, Mrs. Foster," Willie said. In his enthusiasm, he bumped into the cart, leapt to catch the books toppling from the pile, and knocked out a dozen more.

Marla groaned. Mrs. Foster snorted. Nobody laughed. "Sorry," Willie said as he began to pick up the books.

Marla concentrated so hard on shelving books that she didn't stop no matter what Willie did. She didn't think it was funny when Willie pulled an imaginary spider out of her hair. She didn't think it was funny when he screamed in the stacks and came out clutching his throat, claiming a vampire had gotten him. She did smile and shake her head when he tripped over Mrs. Foster's step stool and sprawled in the aisle, but he couldn't take credit for that because it was an accident.

"So that's what makes you laugh," he said after he almost fell. To his amazement tears came to Marla's eyes. Immediately, she ducked her head and went back to work again.

At lunchtime Mrs. Foster sent them off to rejoin their class in the cafeteria.

On the way, Marla surprised him by saying, "I suppose you're going to forget the tape player you said you'd bring to the barn today."

"Uh-uh, I won't forget," Willie said and kicked himself mentally for having temporarily forgotten.

"I found two tapes. My girlfriend gave them to me to keep when I moved away from her."

"Good," he said. "Hey, want me to buy your lunch for you?"

"No, you already gave me a cookie. I'm going to eat that. Thanks, Willie."

"Just one cookie for lunch?"

"I don't eat much. Dancers have to stay thin."

She wasn't thin. She was plump and he liked her that way, but he didn't tell her that. Instead, he went off to buy today's special, beef stew and mashed potatoes, not for the stew, which he wasn't planning to eat, but for the buttery mashed potatoes.

There was no chance to talk to Marla during language arts or social studies. Just before the last bell Willie got an idea and asked to be excused. Mr. Rose, the art teacher, let him go. Mr. Rose was a pretty understanding guy. One time when Willie was in disgrace, Mr. Rose told him that when he was a kid, he'd been a clown in school, too.

"But I grew out of it, and so will you," Mr. Rose had said. Then he'd crossed his eyes and hung his tongue out of the corner of his mouth, leaving Willie laughing and feeling much better.

From Mr. Rose's room, Willie went down to his old first-grade teacher. She was sitting at her desk, as young and pretty as ever, and luckily her kids had already been dismissed so he had her to himself for a few minutes.

"Do you still have the puppet we used in that frog prince play we put on when I was in your class?" he asked.

"I might. What do you need it for?"

"Just for something," he said. "I'll bring it back tomorrow."

She pinched his cheek affectionately. "You better not forget, Willie. That frog's my favorite puppet."

"And you're still my favorite teacher," Willie told her on his way out of her room with the frog puppet.

It was true, too. He'd always had a crush on Mrs. Stezhinewski, even if he'd never been able to pronounce her name.

He hid the puppet by stuffing it down the front of his shirt. It looked a little odd there, but people were so used to him looking odd that no one stared.

After the bell rang, Willie barged out of class, startling Jackson and nearly knocking down Milton, who growled, "Watch it, butt brain."

Willie hid in the bushes by the side door where the bus riders would come out. He had to wait a long time for Marla. When she came out in the last trickle of bus-bound kids, he put his hand into the frog puppet and propped it up on a branch.

"Kiss a frog. Oh, please, pretty lady, this frog needs a kiss so baaad," Willie croaked in a froggy voice.

She jerked to a stop and stared. A little first grader

stopped wide-eyed beside her, then scooted off, scared. Marla narrowed her eyes and asked, "What would I want to kiss a frog for?"

"Because," Willie said, still croaking, "you never know what might happen. Try it. You'll like it."

"Not if *you're* going to turn out to be the prince, Willie."

He made the frog double over and croak pitifully, "Nobody loves me because I'm green and warty. But underneath I'm such a nice guy."

"Oh, you!" Marla said. "You're so goofy." She gave the frog puppet a quick kiss.

Willie leapt up from the bush, eyes crossed like Mr. Rose's. "Thank you, princess," he shouted. "Now that you've released me from the evil spell, I am yours to command."

"As long as I don't have to kiss *you*," Marla said. But it tickled him to see her smiling. He went home feeling good, without a thought of his father, or Boo-boo, or concentrating, or any other kind of trouble.

8

The Big
Father-Son Project

*B*ooboo's joyous greeting always made Willie feel like a returning hero. He'd jump on Willie, barking and licking his face, even knocking him down— not to mention getting muddy paw marks on his jacket if the yard was wet. But today Booboo wasn't in the yard.

In the kitchen, nothing more exuberant than the humming refrigerator awaited Willie. "Willie, that you?" Dad called from the living room.

"Yes, Dad. Where's Booboo?" Willie stopped at the edge of the living room carpet.

"Locked in the basement. He dug his way out of the yard. I caught him terrorizing the mailman. I'm enrolling that dog in the next session of obedience training school."

"He flunked out, Dad. Don't you remember? Mom took him last year."

"Yes, well, this time *I'm* taking him—after we finish the doghouse. You ready to start on it?" Dad sounded eager.

"Sure." But the sound of his dog woofing in the basement made Willie ask, "Dad, what if Booboo flunks out again?"

"You mean if he's untrainable? Then we get rid of him, Willie. But don't worry; your dog's not going back to the pound yet."

Willie shuddered. This was the second time Dad had mentioned getting rid of Booboo. "I gotta go to my room, Dad," Willie mumbled. "Be right back."

He retreated to his room and slumped onto his bed. His stomach felt queasy. Maybe he was getting sick. Whatever—he needed to feel better before working on the doghouse or he'd mess up and make Dad angry.

Lying there, Willie started thinking about the responsibility test Dad had given him last spring after Mom had finally convinced Dad that a dog would be good for Willie. For two weeks Willie had to remember on his own to do his homework, set the table, and take out the garbage. Mom had kept him from flunking the test by secretly reminding him now and then.

At the end of the two weeks, she had said to Dad, "See? See what your son can do?"

That evening Dad had brought home a pile of books on dogs from the library and read aloud to them about German shepherds and what good watch-dogs they make. "Willie wants a pet," Mom had said. "If you want a watchdog, Harold, get one for yourself."

"I can't understand why you went to the pound for a dog when you never hesitate to buy the best in anything else," Dad had said when they brought home Booboo.

"We didn't plan to get a dog there. We just went to see what kind of dog Willie liked," Mom had explained.

"And you got *no* kind," Dad had said.

It was useless to remind Dad about how funny and lovable Booboo was. Funny and lovable didn't count for much with Dad. Mom often called Willie lovable. But he suspected Dad wouldn't have picked either him or Booboo if he'd had a choice.

Mom claimed Dad loved him. "Your father can't say it, but it's there," she said. "He may criticize you, but he loves you. Believe me, Willie."

But what if she was wrong? Suppose Dad didn't really love him. Then he might not put up with Boo-boo's mistakes. Then, unless the dog started behaving, Booboo really would be in danger.

"Willie." Dad walked in without knocking. "What are you doing? Change your clothes, and come down to the garage immediately."

Willie took a deep breath and let it out slowly. "Where's Mom?"

"She went to visit a friend." Dad puffed out his lower lip and admitted, "She said I made her nervous."

You make me nervous, too, Willie wanted to say, but with Booboo's life at stake, he only ventured, "I don't need to change my clothes. These are my old jeans."

"Then let's get started," Dad said.

He had all the materials laid out and ready to go in the garage. "Now, the first thing I want you to do is mark these boards for where I need to cut them on my bench saw. Don't get too near the bench saw. It's dangerous." Nothing new in that warning. He had always told Willie to keep away from the tools. Willie wasn't even allowed to use one of Dad's hammers.

"First, look at the drawing and read off the measurements for the long boards that go on the side of the house," Dad said.

Willie's throat tightened the way it did when he was taking a test, but he managed to figure out which measurement to read. "Four feet six inches."

"Good. Now, you hold the end of my steel rule." Dad pulled out the metal tape until he had the right length. He began marking the boards.

Willie held and watched. "Don't you want me to mark the boards?" he asked. He figured doing something would help him concentrate.

"Let me show you how it should be done first. These measurements need to be exact. An eighth of an inch either way and the seams won't be tight. Just watch me, and then you can do the next one."

Willie held. Willie watched. Dad marked the four feet six inches by drawing a line with a T square. "See? Have to make sure the line is straight," Dad said. He did another board to make doubly sure Willie got the idea. Willie watched. After the third board, when Dad was making triply sure, Willie's mind slid sideways and wandered away.

It took him by surprise when Dad finally said, "Your turn."

Willie picked up the pencil and the steel rule gingerly.

"Now don't let go of the end," Dad said, making Willie jump so that the narrow steel ribbon slid off the board.

"Hang onto it," Dad snapped.

Willie tried again. Shakily, he drew the line on the board with the T square.

"You're not holding the square right," Dad said. "It should butt up against the board exactly to make your line perpendicular. Let me show you once more."

Feeling stupid, Willie watched his father draw the line. He shifted from one foot to the other, remembering that Booboo was still down in the basement. "Dad, can I let Booboo up now?"

"No. Pay attention now, Willie."

Willie thought he could hear his heart jittering in

his chest. For a while he listened to it, wondering if he was going to die. Finally, Dad drew the lines to his own satisfaction. He started up the bench saw. "Remember, don't get too close to this saw," Dad said again.

That was when his promise to Marla popped into Willie's mind. "I have to go now, Dad," he yelled over the scream of the saw. "Someone's waiting for me."

"Let them wait."

"But I promised I'd bring them my tape player. They need to use it."

"What?" Dad turned off the saw, and Willie repeated what he'd said. "You should never lend things like a tape player. It's bound to get broken," Dad said. "Go phone them and say you're busy and can't come."

"But I don't know their number."

"Then you'll have to wait until you see them again to explain. . . . Who is it, anyway?"

"A new friend from school."

"You knew we were going to work on this doghouse. Why did you make an appointment when you know you have to leave your afternoons free until we finish?"

"But I forgot, Dad, and I promised, and—"

Dad frowned in irritation. "How many times have I told you to carry a pocket calendar and write things down? What did you do with the pocket calendar I gave you in September?"

Willie shrugged, blinking helplessly.

"Lost it? You'd lose your head if it wasn't attached. Well, use your school notebook to keep track of your responsibilities, then."

That finished the discussion as far as Dad was concerned. He flipped the switch on the bench saw and picked up the first board. "Hold this end, Willie. Don't push it or put any pressure on it. Just hold it while I guide it through."

Numbly, Willie held the board.

"I told you not to put pressure on it."

"I'm not, Dad."

"Yes, you are."

The board dropped. "HOLD IT!" Dad yelled.

Willie jumped.

Dad looked weary after he had cut the boards. "This is going to take us longer than I thought. And today was just the easy part," he said.

Willie imagined the rest of December, and then Christmas vacation, passing while he held up heavy boards with his fingertips and Dad yelled at him for doing it wrong. And what for? So Booboo could shiver miserably out in the doghouse in the winter cold.

A pathetic yowl from the basement went straight to Willie's heart.

Mom's car pulled up in front of the open garage. Dad was using her parking space for the bench saw. "My, my, my," she said out the car window. "Look at you two covered in sawdust."

She stepped out of the car, keeping well away from the pale particles blanketing the area in front of her. "Are you having fun?" She laughed and took several shopping bags from the trunk.

"What did you buy?" Dad asked, brushing sawdust from his rolled-up sleeves.

"Nothing major; just this and that. . . . I'll have dinner ready in a half hour. Or are you too busy to eat?"

"Is it dinnertime?" Dad sounded surprised. Willie wasn't. He was tired enough for it to have been bedtime.

Mom turned to Willie. "Come in and tell me how your day was, sweet stuff. . . . After you clean up."

Willie looked at Dad, who told him gruffly, "Go ahead and help your mother. I'll clean up here by myself."

That made Willie feel guilty, and he hesitated. But when Mom tugged at his sleeve, he followed her into the house.

"What's that noise?" she asked.

"Dad locked Booboo in the basement."

"Well, let him out. I'm sure he's been there long enough."

Willie opened the door at the head of the basement

stairs and whistled. Booboo came to the foot of the stairs and looked up hopefully. When he saw it was Willie, he bounded up, barking hysterically. It took fifteen minutes before he stopped leaping and barking and calmed down enough to drink some water and eat some doggy treats.

"It's okay, Booboo, it's okay. I know it wasn't fun down there, but you're free now," Willie said.

Meanwhile, Mom was putting salmon steak in the broiler and cutting up salad. "Having your father home is hard for all of us," she said. "But it's hardest for him. He's really worried about his job. It would be tough to get another one as good at his age, and it's possible his boss *might* get mad enough to fire him."

"But Dad's the best engineer in the world."

"Probably. He still might get fired, though. So you be patient with him, Willie. Okay?"

"Yeah," Willie said. "I'll try. . . . Mom," he said, "I promised this girl I'd bring her my tape player so she could dance to it, but Dad won't let me."

"A girl? You have a girlfriend?" Mom sounded delighted.

"She isn't my girlfriend," Willie said. "She already thinks I'm a goofball, and now she'll be mad at me about the tape player."

"Call her and apologize."

"I don't know her telephone number."

"What's her last name?"

"I forget. She's new."

"Well, where does she live?"

"I don't know the address exactly."

"Oh, Willie!" Mom laughed. "What a way to conduct your love life. Tell you what. You send her a note in school and invite her here and we can lend her the tape player together."

Willie smiled and gave her a quick hug. "Did I ever tell you what a great mom you are?" he asked.

"Uh-huh," she said, hugging him back, "but I love to hear it."

He set the table feeling much better. He even got the forks on the left and the knives and spoons on the right and lined them up with the bottom of the plate the way Dad liked it. He almost forgot the napkins, though. Napkins were so forgettable. He could just imagine Dad noticing and saying his favorite line, "Willie'd forget his head if it wasn't attached."

If only Dad would forget what he'd said about Booboo. But Dad was a man who never forgot anything. Worse yet, once he made up his mind, even Mom couldn't always make him change it.

9

Sewer Pipe Caper

*B*ooboo scratched at the storm door and yowled inquiringly a couple of times during dinner. Willie had to keep hopping up to tell him that they'd go for a walk soon, in a little while, just another minute. "Be patient, Booboo." The dog's intelligent brown eyes took in every word, but he didn't understand why he had to wait.

"Don't go out of the development," Dad said after Willie stacked the dirty dishes for Mom and got Booboo's leash. "And take a flashlight."

"I don't need one," Willie said.

"It's dark out," Dad fretted in his usual worrywart way.

"Willie will be fine," Mom said. "Young eyes can see in the dark. And he has Booboo to protect him." She winked at Willie. They both knew that Booboo would put his tail between his legs and hide behind Willie if anything seemed threatening. Furthermore, he greeted all strangers with a wagging tail. Except mailmen. Something about mailmen irked Booboo.

The winter dark was thick under an overcast sky, and it had turned chilly. Willie could feel the cold even in his down ski parka because, as usual, he hadn't worn hat or gloves. Still, he was glad to be outdoors and away from his father's all-seeing eye. "He can't help being a perfectionist," Mom had told Willie. "He was born that way." But Willie remembered a story Dad had told him about his father, who died before Willie was born.

It seems Dad's father had given him an erector set when he was six, and Dad had built a bridge with it. He had been so proud of himself for handling all those little screws and bolts that the minute his father got home from work, he had shown him the bridge. One nudge from his father's foot and the bridge fell apart.

Next day Dad had built another bridge, tightening the screws better this time. Again his father had pushed at the crucial point and collapsed it. The third bridge had stood. From that, Dad claimed, he had learned that anything worth doing had to be done just right. What Willie learned was that his grandfather had been pretty mean. He admired his father for not giving up. If it had been him, Willie was pretty sure he just would have decided he wasn't a good enough builder and stopped playing with the erector set.

Down the paved road past three colonials, two split-levels, and one bare modern house was the red fireplug that Booboo liked best. He took his time sniffing around the base of it, his plumy tail up like a scythe, before he lifted his leg to relieve himself.

"Let's walk to where the highway department's putting in storm sewers and see how they're doing," Willie suggested. The big sewer pipe sections parked at the entrance to their development were fun to sit in. From inside the sewer pipe, the sounds of cars passing on the county road echoed eerily. Dad had said that the ground was going to be too frozen to work if the highway department didn't get the storm sewers in soon. Even when the winters weren't snowy here in Niskayuna, New York, they were cold.

Today, Willie was surprised to see his classmate Milton, and Milton's pal Patrick, fooling around with the pipes. Skinny Patrick was standing on top of a pipe, holding up a stick as if he meant to whack it down on something that might crawl out of the end. Milton appeared to be guarding the other end of the pipe. When Willie got a little closer, he saw a figure crouched inside it. Jackson?

"Hey, Jackson," Willie called, "what're you doing?"

"I was riding my bike, and these guys took me prisoner," Jackson said.

Willie noticed the bike lying near the roadside.

"We're going to roll him into a ditch and bury him if he don't come out," Milton said. "Why don't you call him to come out and play, Willie?"

"Not me. I got better things to do."

"Like what?" Milton demanded. Patrick turned around to look at Willie, leaving his end of the pipe unwatched.

"Well—" Willie searched frantically for an idea that would help Jackson get away. "I was thinking about making like an obstacle course with those pipes." It was a notion he'd considered when he first saw the big, hollow cylinders. "You know, standing them on end in the road so the cars would have to drive around them to get into the development?"

Milton cocked his head and looked interested. Meanwhile, Jackson took the opportunity to sneak quietly out of the pipe. "Not bad," Milton said. "We set them up, then hide and watch the fun, huh?"

"Yeah," Willie said. "There'll be lots of traffic into the development in the next hour, with people coming home from work and this being the only way in."

Milton laughed. "Right. They'll go crazy honking their horns."

"I'M GOING TO TELL MY DAD WHAT YOU DID TO ME, MILTON," Jackson yelled from a safe distance across the county road.

"We didn't do nothing. We were just teasing, you big sissy," Milton yelled back. Jackson made an obscene gesture and started running. Jackson was a very good runner. At spring track and field day, he'd come in first every year.

"Boy, has he got a short fuse. All we were doing was trying to scare him a little," Milton said. It was possible, Willie thought, but with Milton, you could never be sure how far the teasing would go.

"Come on, Willie. We gotta get this obstacle course set up quick before he sics his father on us," Milton said.

"He left his bike," Patrick said.

"I'll keep it for him," Willie said. "I'll take it home right now." Now that Jackson was free, Willie had lost interest in the obstacle course. But Milton wasn't about to let him go.

"Right now you got to help with these pipes," Milton said. "They weigh a ton. Come on. This one first."

Booboo didn't like helping with the pipes. He pulled against the leash and yipped. "Tie him up somewhere," Milton commanded.

Willie tied Booboo to a telephone pole. Booboo lay down and rested his head on his paws. He watched them wistfully.

A car drove past as they were rolling the third pipe into place. It slowed but didn't stop. The driver had no trouble weaving her way through the obstacle course. It was the last two pipes which they upended in midroad that made the course tricky.

Milton said, "Time to get out of sight. Where can we hide, Willie?"

Willie suggested the side of a house whose windows were still dark, which must mean the owners hadn't come home yet. When Willie and Milton and Patrick took cover alongside the house, Booboo sat up. He lifted his head and barked. "I better get him," Willie said.

"No," Milton said. "He'll give us away. Leave him there."

Booboo barked louder. It kept getting darker. The few driveway lampposts that were lit shone palely over dead brown gardens. Willie wanted badly to take Booboo and go home.

"I better get Jackson's bike before someone steals it," Willie said.

"Who cares about Jackson's bike? Let him come back and get it himself," Milton said.

"No, I think I'll just—"

Milton elbowed Willie in the stomach hard. "Cool it," he said. "Here they come."

Three cars turned into the development and halted, one behind the other. A man got out of the first car and asked in a loud, angry voice what was going on here. Patrick snickered. The man tried to move an upended sewer pipe by pushing it. It didn't budge. A second man got out of his station wagon and joined the first. Then the third person, a woman, got out of her Jeep. The three of them questioned each other about whether the highway department had gone crazy.

"Whoever did this, I gotta get home," the first man said. He and the second man, who was small and fat, tipped the sewer pipe section. The woman helped them lower it to its side so it could be rolled out of the way. They moved the two other sections of pipe the same way, got back in their cars, and drove past.

"That wasn't much fun," Milton said.

"No, I guess it wasn't such a good idea," Willie agreed. He didn't care. At least it had given Jackson a chance to escape. "Well, see you," Willie said casually. He went to untie his dog and pick up Jackson's bike, but just as he put his hands on the bike, a police car pulled up.

"You!" the policeman said. "Hold it right there."

Willie looked around. Neither Milton nor Patrick was in sight. The policeman had to be talking to him. "I didn't do it," Willie said.

It didn't help that Booboo suddenly turned vicious and tried to bite the policeman's leg. "Tie that dog up out of the way," the policeman ordered. He looked so much like Jackson that Willie guessed he must be Jackson's father, whom he'd never met. Jackson's mother had been the only one around whenever Willie had visited.

Booboo howled when he found himself tied to the

lamppost again. He was really tired of that lamppost. "It's all right, Booboo. You're going home soon," Willie promised.

He returned to the policeman and said, "I guess you came because Jackson told you some kids were teasing him, but—"

"What's your name, kid?"

"Willie. Willie Feldman. I'm Jackson's friend. That's why I was picking up his bike."

"We'll see about that." The policeman didn't look up from the pad he was busy writing on. Wasn't he Jackson's father? Or was it that he didn't believe Willie?

"Address," the policeman said. Willie told it to him. "Get in the squad car" was the next command.

"Are you taking me to jail? I didn't do anything," Willie cried.

"I want to have a talk with your parents, William Feldman."

"What about my dog?"

"Someone from the pound can come pick him up. Let's go." Jackson's father piled the bike in the back of the squad car and put Willie in front, leaving Booboo tied where he was. "Please," Willie begged. "I'll do anything. Don't let them take my dog to the pound. My dad's already mad at him."

"Take it easy," the policeman said and put the car in gear.

"But I'm Jackson's friend," Willie wailed. "Why won't you believe me?"

By the time the squad car pulled into his driveway, Willie was frantic. He couldn't decide which was worse—Booboo's winding up at the pound or him being delivered to his father by a policeman.

At the sight of the policeman ringing the front doorbell, Willie panicked. He leapt from the squad car and ran. He ran wildly, arms flailing, back to the scene of the crime he hadn't committed. At least he hadn't committed the one the policeman thought he had. He'd just kind of suggested the sewer pipe barricade. Was that a crime?

He'd only been trying to help Jackson. But Dad would say he should have thought through the idea before mentioning it to Milton. Not thinking things through was another of Willie's faults, according to Dad. If Dad had been disgusted with him before for not holding a piece of wood steady enough, what was he going to be like now when he found out his goofup son was a criminal?

Booboo barked a greeting, and his tail started to wag as soon as he saw Willie coming. Willie untied him from the lamppost, thinking about where to hide. The sewer pipe section, of course! From there Willie could see the moon and the headlights of passing cars. It was a peaceful spot, and after all the running he'd done, Willie was in need of some rest.

What woke him up was the cold. How long had he been asleep, he wondered. Booboo was whimpering in his sleep, having bad dreams. His head rested on Willie's leg. Willie crawled out of the sewer pipe and led Booboo home. He was relieved to find no police car waiting there to haul him off to jail.

Now to sneak quietly into the house. But the instant he opened the side door, Dad walked into the kitchen and Mom promptly squeezed in after him. She got to Willie first and enveloped him in her warm arms. "Are you all right, my angel boy?"

"I'm fine, Mom. Just cold." Willie's teeth were chattering.

"Sit down. I'll make you some hot cocoa."

"What do you have to say for yourself?" Dad asked.

"I'm sorry," Willie said.

"You better be. That policeman said he never had a kid escape from a squad car before."

"I think the policeman was Jackson's father. I told him who I was."

"He said he thought you knew his son."

"Oh, gee. I didn't have to escape then."

"You also didn't have to obstruct traffic with those sewer pipe sections," Dad said. "That was the complaint Jackson's father was answering when he found you. You might have been charged with malicious mischief for that, Willie."

"Well, but I was trying to give the kids that were teasing Jackson something else fun to do so they'd let him alone."

"Was that really your intention?" Dad asked.

"Harold! What a question!" Mom said. "Of *course* Willie tried to save his friend. He stands up for what's right, just like you do."

"Did you, Willie?"

"Yes, Dad. I guess it wasn't a great idea, but it was the best I could come up with then."

"It was a harebrained scheme, and trying to escape punishment by running away from the law was worse," Dad said. "I don't know, Willie." Dad shook his head. Everybody took a minute out to watch Booboo lapping up water as if he hadn't had a drink in days.

"Don't let the cocoa boil over," Dad finally said to Mom. He seemed to be done yelling at Willie.

This time he had gotten off easy, Willie thought with relief. He put down his cocoa and asked, "Dad, about the doghouse, could I please have tomorrow afternoon off from building it?"

"What for?"

"I need to do something." Willie was hoping that if he explained what had happened, Marla would forgive him for being one day late.

"I don't think that your behavior warrants—" Dad began.

"Harold, let me speak to you a moment," Mom said. She grabbed her husband by the arm and tugged him out of the kitchen.

Willie heard her fierce whispering without understanding it, but when she stuck her head back into the kitchen she said, "It's okay for tomorrow afternoon. Good luck."

There was no doubt about it, Willie thought gratefully. He had the best mother in the world.

10

Getting in the Game

*B*y the time Willie got to school the next morning, he had rehearsed his excuse for not bringing the tape deck to Marla so often that the words were like a rain cloud ready to burst. Even when he didn't see Marla in homeroom, he kept muttering his excuse to himself. He watched the door and muttered and fidgeted, sure she would show up any minute.

Mrs. Tealso noticed the fidgeting. "Willie, do you need to be excused?" she asked.

"No, Mrs. Tealso. I don't have to go."

"Then for heaven's sake, sit still," she said. Later, despite her annoyance with him, she stopped beside his desk and said quietly, "I'm going to be working in my room after school if you'd like some help with your math."

"Thanks for the offer, Mrs. Tealso, but I'm sort of

busy this afternoon," Willie said. Her sigh filled him with guilt, but the next instant he was back thinking about Marla.

Why hadn't she come to school? Was she sick? . . . Unless she had to take care of her mother. Boy, she must be angry that he hadn't kept his promise.

"Willie, didn't you hear the bell?" Mrs. Tealso asked. "You're supposed to be in science."

"Oh, sure. I'm on my way." To impress the teacher, he left rapidly, so rapidly that he forgot his book bag.

Mrs. Tealso was giving her other language arts section their instructions when Willie returned for his bag. He tiptoed in so as not to disturb the silence, but then, "Whoops," he tripped over a chair leg. "I'm sorry, Mrs. Tealso," Willie said over the class's laughter. She raised an eyebrow and pointed at the door. He grabbed his bag and slunk away.

At lunch Willie sat across from Jackson, whose round, innocent face was lit by a smile. "I was sure wrong about *you,* Willie," Jackson said. "You're tough enough for girls to like."

"I am?"

"Yeah. You stood up to Milton for me. That kid's such a pain."

"When he's teasing he is. Watch it. Here he comes."

"Anybody sitting with you guys?" Milton asked.

"No," Willie said.

"Good. Me and Patrick'll join you." Milton dropped his heavy-duty hulk into a seat next to Jackson, who immediately began edging his chair away. Patrick sat down beside Willie.

"So how come you're not in jail?" Milton asked Willie as he removed a plastic-wrapped bologna and cheese sandwich from his lunch bag.

"I didn't do anything wrong," Willie said.

"Yeah, but that cop didn't know that. I bet you told him I did it."

"No. I didn't tell him anything."

"So how come he didn't take you in?" Milton asked.

"Yeah, how come?" Patrick echoed.

"I escaped," Willie said. Suddenly he spotted Marla entering the cafeteria. She sat down by herself at the garbage pail table. Her head was hanging so low that hair was all Willie could see above her neck.

"No kidding?" Milton sounded impressed. "How'd you do that?"

"I jumped out of the squad car. . . . Excuse me," Willie said. "I got to talk to someone." Abruptly he stood up and crossed the room to Marla. He could feel the boys' eyes on him, but he didn't care.

"Marla, about the tape player," he began when he got to her table. "I didn't forget it. But see, my father's making me help him build a doghouse because Booboo wet on his puzzle. So—but I'll bring the tape player to the barn today. Okay?"

Her expression went from cloudy to sunlit. "It's okay about the tape player, Willie. I can't go to the barn today anyway. I'm going to stay after school so Mrs. Tealso can help me with the math I've missed."

"Gee," he said. He was so relieved that she wasn't angry that he added on impulse, "Maybe I'll stay after school, too. I need lots of help with my math." They'd be alone in the classroom, he thought, just Marla and him and Mrs. Tealso.

"Suit yourself, Willie."

She hadn't invited him to sit down, and her face had clouded over again. He guessed she wanted him to leave her alone. "Yeah," he said. "Well, see you then." He returned to his table and his unfinished lunch.

"So you got a girlfriend, huh?" Milton sounded impressed.

"She's not my girlfriend," Willie said. "I don't even know if she likes me."

"Oh yeah? Well, that's how it goes, kid." Milton offered him a pickle. Willie shook his head. "The girls you like don't like you back, and you don't like the ones that like you," Milton said. "That's what my big brother says, and he's got plenty of experience."

"Your big brother works at the body shop on Nott Terrace, doesn't he?" Jackson asked.

"Yeah. How do you know?" Milton asked.

"I saw him there. He looks just like you."

"Yeah." Milton sounded flattered. "And we both

look like my dad. You know him? He works for the highway department."

Jackson shook his head and asked, "Does everybody in your family pump iron?"

"Everybody but my mom," Milton said. "I got Patrick working out with me, too. Patrick, show them your muscle." Patrick exhibited a walnut-sized bicep. They examined it respectfully. "You guys could come over after school if you want," Milton said. "We got a regular gym in the basement—weights, a life cycle machine, and a trampoline."

"Thanks, but I'm busy building a doghouse," Willie said.

"So how long can it take to build a little doghouse? Come over tomorrow or the next day."

"This doghouse could last until Christmas—maybe longer," Willie said. "See, my father's building it, and he does things perfect."

"You didn't come out so perfect," Milton said, and he laughed as if he'd said something funny.

Willie grinned. He knew how far from perfect he was. "Do you like doing things with your father, Milton?" he asked.

"Yeah, Pop's a great guy."

"My dad's a great guy too," Willie said loyally. But he wondered if, after they finished the doghouse, training Booboo would be the next father-son project. Considering how happy-go-lucky Booboo was, training him could take until Willie got to high school, or maybe beyond—if Booboo didn't get sent back to the pound first.

The lunch period was long enough so that kids who wanted to go out to the ball field could do so for the last twenty minutes. Milton was one of the two permanently elected lunchtime softball captains.

"Want to be on my team?" Milton asked Willie and Jackson. Willie gaped, overwhelmed at being asked. Milton had never asked him before. In fact he'd never accepted Willie on his team without a lot of groaning and insults.

"He thinks you're tough because you got away with last night," Jackson whispered in Willie's ear as they followed Milton outside. "You wouldn't have if I hadn't talked to my father after he got home. I told him it was Milton and Patrick set up those pipes. I was afraid they'd steal my bike. And I told Pop you saved me."

"Thanks," Willie said.

"Well, you did save me." Jackson gave him a friendly sock on the shoulder before running out to take his usual place in the infield.

Milton put Willie off in right field.

Willie liked softball. He could connect with the ball most times when he was up at bat. His only problem was out in the field. If the ball didn't come his way for a while, he'd start thinking about something and forget to catch it.

He was thinking about how his plans for the afternoon had gotten messed up and wondering if staying to get help with math was better or worse than going home and holding things for Dad. Neither sounded like much fun. He thought about the tape deck. Maybe he should leave it in the barn for Marla, or maybe on the porch of that old house near the barn, which was probably where she lived since it was the only house near the barn.

"Willie, catch the *ballllll*!" came Milton's shouted command from across the field.

Willie's hand jerked up automatically. Thunk, came the ball right at his palm. It bounced off but he picked it up. He was grinning in disbelief at the ball in his hand when Milton winged another command at him.

"Throw it to second, Willie. To *seeeecond*."

Willie threw, putting the man—or girl, in this case—out. Milton thumped him on the back after the game was over. "Good hustle, Willie."

Willie was thrilled. Never mind the D Mrs. Tealso gave him in paragraph construction, or the disappointing grade in the math quiz because his five somehow looked like a three. He'd gotten a man out for Milton. What's more, Jackson had called him tough. Maybe being a goofup wasn't necessarily a permanent condition.

He presented himself at his homeroom door after the last bell rang and asked, "Can I stay after with Marla and learn some math too, Mrs. Tealso?"

She blinked her eyes at him in surprise. "Why, Willie, of course you can stay." Then she frowned. "So long as you don't disturb Marla."

There was no chance of that. During the hour in which Mrs. Tealso unraveled the mysteries of solving word problems for them, Marla never took her eyes off the teacher except to write answers on her work sheets. For all the good it did Willie to be in the same room with Marla, he might as well have gone home. That girl sure could concentrate, Willie thought. Even Dad would be impressed.

11

Lucky Day

*T*he minute Willie hopped off the late school bus and stepped into the kitchen he asked his mother, "Did Booboo do anything bad today?"

"No, Booboo's doing fine. But your mother's not." She was bouncing energetically as she chopped up vegetables on the butcher block. Usually Mom kissed him hello when he got home from school, but today she hadn't even stopped to look at him.

Willie was alarmed. "What's wrong?"

"Your father is driving me *crazy*. I can't stay in this house with him watching every move I make. I'm thinking of visiting my aunt in Brooklyn for a few days."

"You are? What about me?"

"Oh, Willie! You can't come. You'd miss too much schoolwork."

He guessed by her flushed, wild look that she

hadn't made up her mind yet. She was just upset and tossing out possibilities. "Why're you mad at Dad?" he asked.

"I'm not mad. I'm *furious*. You know what he did?" Mom's eyes flashed as they met Willie's. "He put me on an allowance. That makes me a child like you, Willie. We both have to ask him, please, for our allowance."

She returned to attacking the onions and peppers so fiercely that some bounced off the block into the sink. "And all because I bought a warm-up suit on sale. Don't I realize he might lose his job, he says to me. As if we don't have money enough saved to carry us for years! As if some of that money wasn't contributed by me."

"Where's Dad now?"

"Off buying nails that won't rust. He's building Booboo a doghouse that will outlast us all."

"Mom, Booboo's going to hate being stuck outside."

"You think I don't know that? Booboo's like me. He needs companionship. And to put that poor animal out in December—" She sighed elaborately. "If only they'd call and ask your father to come back to work, we'd all be happy again. He hates being home. Building doghouses! He's driving himself crazy, too."

"Couldn't you phone his office and tell them to call him?"

"Butt into your father's business? He'd kill me."

She stared at Willie and puffed out her cheeks, thinking. Suddenly her eyes twinkled with mischief. "If he caught me, he'd kill me, but why should he catch me? Especially if I just hint around a tiny little bit. Say I call his secretary and have a cosy chat, hmmm? Tell her how sick Harold is of this so-called vacationing."

She kissed Willie with a loud smack, "Mwah," right on the lips. "You're so smart," she said, giving him full credit for the idea.

She was already on the phone when Willie got Booboo's leash and collected him from the backyard. Booboo was shivering. He pulled toward the house, but Willie explained that they had to check out the spiderwebs in the barn. "Come on," he said. "Walking will warm you up, Booboo."

Reluctantly, Booboo let himself be dragged toward the street. Once at his fireplug, he forgot to be miserable. Up went his tail. Jauntily, he led the way toward the barn.

The sky was clotted with clouds, but the chilly air seemed to threaten more snow than rain. Willie thought of the snowboard he'd gotten for Christmas last year. Riding it down the golf course hill, he'd felt like a surfer scudding down a gigantic wave. But naturally, since he didn't know how to surfboard, he'd fallen. When he got home with the blood running into his eye, Mom had taken him to be stitched up in the emergency room, and after that Dad had laid down the law. No snowboarding without a crash helmet. Never mind that nobody else wore a crash helmet; Willie must wear one. Dad even took Willie out that very evening to buy him a helmet at the sporting goods store.

Willie still had it in the closet with his skateboard and hockey stick and skates and boogie board. He had a lot of gear that he didn't get to use very much, mostly because every time he fell or banged himself up a little, Dad put restrictions on where and when he could do things. Willie had pointed out that he couldn't be perfect at something the first time he tried it, but Dad had just said, "You wouldn't be so imperfect if you'd approach things cautiously. You don't have to go down the steepest hill the first time."

"It's because your father is afraid something might happen to you, Willie," Mom had explained to him. "You're a miracle to him, you know."

"I am?"

"Of course you are. His first wife couldn't have children, and he'd given up hope before he married me. When you were born, he went around grinning for months."

"He did? You mean he liked me when I was born? Wow!" Willie said.

He had been impressed enough to wear the helmet a few times for his father's sake, but then one afternoon he'd forgotten it. That day the skiing had been so perfect on the crystalline snow under the sapphire sky that he'd babbled at dinner about what a great time he'd had. Next thing he knew, Dad asked if he'd worn his helmet, and when Willie admitted he hadn't, Dad stowed the board in his car trunk. As far as Willie knew, it was still there.

Too bad he couldn't make himself lie to his father, or keep his mouth shut, at least. Life would be easier if he could lie. It seemed that even his good points—like being honest—got him in trouble with Dad.

Booboo barked and pulled at the leash as they walked past the deserted house. Judging by the smoke coming from the chimney, it wasn't deserted anymore. Booboo stood up, managing to wag his tail furiously and balance on his hind legs at the same time. Then Willie saw what excited him. Marla was coming around the side of the house with an armload of wood.

"Marla!" he called in happy surprise. "Hey, Marla, it's me, Willie."

"Are you going to the barn?"

"Yeah," he said. "Wanna come with me?"

"I can't. Mom's sick in bed, and the stove's about out of wood again. It keeps the house plenty warm for her, but it gobbles wood like crazy." She set the load down on the porch. "Dad spends every minute after work bringing in wood. We don't even read to each other at night anymore because he's too pooped to keep his eyes open."

"I could help you," Willie said. "I'd like to help you, Marla."

She considered. "Okay, I guess. If you don't mind." She gave Booboo the hugs he was pestering her for before she led Willie to the backyard. It was bare with patchy grass, and behind it, next to a garage, stood a railroad car–sized stack of firewood.

"Wow!" Willie said. "You've got enough to heat your house for the whole winter there."

"That's why my father took this place. So we'd save on fuel bills. Otherwise the house is awful. It's so musty. Mom thinks that may be what brought back her headaches."

"Can't a doctor cure them?"

"They haven't yet. . . . If only they would and she could go back to teaching! When I was little, Mom taught and Dad stayed home to write—he'd like to be a novelist. That was before we started moving around so much, when I had the girlfriend who gave me the dance tapes."

"Gee, I'm sorry about the tape player, Marla. You want to come to my house and we'll get it?"

"No, I couldn't do that."

"You're still mad at me for not bringing it?"

"I'm not mad at you, Willie. How could I be when you're so nice to me? And nobody else is in this school—except Mrs. Tealso. But I need a girlfriend, and you're a boy."

"You don't like boys?"

"Well—I mean. Urrrr." She bared her teeth in frustration. "I can't explain what I mean. Except I need someone I can talk to."

"Why can't you talk to me?"

She stared at him, and her face went through a whole film clip of emotions from thoughtful to amused. "I guess I *am* talking to you, aren't I?" she said finally. Then she laughed.

He was delighted to have made her laugh although he didn't have a clue as to how he'd done it.

"Come on," she said. "Let's stack a pile of wood on the porch, and then I'll ask my mother if she feels okay enough to meet you."

Willie was so pleased at the invitation that he staggered under an extra-heavy, double armload of wood, struggling not to drop any all the way to the front of the house. Concentrate, he told himself in his father's voice. He was determined to do this job right for Marla. Back and forth, back and forth—he was sure he'd moved a forest's worth of wood by the time Marla said, "I guess that's enough for the night."

He couldn't smell the mustiness inside the house because of the apple-sweet smell of the wood burning in the open-fronted stove, but he could see the house wasn't any pleasanter inside than out. The front room, where Marla left him when she went to speak to her mother, was full of unpacked boxes. On one side of the big, black wood stove that heated the house was a couch and a chair, with a stack of books on a table between them. On the other side of the wood stove was a refrigerator, a kitchen sink, and a dining room table and chairs. The only house as primitive as this Willie had ever been in was a cabin in a state park that his family had rented for a week one summer. He wished he could give Marla not only his tape player but anything he owned that would make her life better.

He was still standing exactly where she had left him, facing the fiery maw of the wood stove, when she came back followed by a small, plump woman with Marla's wildly waving hair. The woman looked pale and ill, but lovely, even in the bulky man's bathrobe she was wearing.

"This is Willie, Mom," Marla said.

"I wanted to thank you for being so kind to my daughter, Willie," Marla's mother said. She reached for the back of the armchair as if she needed the support. "Marla dreads going into a new school. She's shy, you know, and it's hard for her to make friends."

"Mom!" Marla objected.

"Well, there's no shame in it, Marla," her mother said. "I'm sure Willie understands."

Willie nodded speechlessly.

"I can see by your face that you're a nice boy. Why don't you offer Willie some—some cocoa, Marla? We have cocoa left, don't we?"

"Dad said he'd do the food shopping on his way

home from work," Marla said. "We're out of milk, Mom."

"Oh, well." Marla's mother put her hand to her head. "See what else we have to offer him. I think I'd better get back to bed. It was nice meeting you, Willie. You come back soon, hear?" She tottered off to her bedroom without waiting for his response.

"Thanks," he called after her. "I'd like to."

"Shush," Marla said putting her finger to her lip. "You have to talk very softly or it hurts her head."

"Gee," he said. "I'm really sorry. She's nice, Marla, and she looks just like you."

Marla smiled. "You should meet her when she's feeling good. She's wonderful then. But I really don't have anything good to offer you to eat, Willie."

"Oh, you don't have to give me anything. I've got to get home to dinner anyway," he said quickly. "I'll come tomorrow and help you stack some more wood. Okay?"

"You don't have to, Willie."

"I want to," he said.

She smiled a toothy, spectacular smile that made her face sparkle. "If you bring your tape player tomorrow, maybe we can go to the barn and dance," she said. "Depending on if I can leave Mom."

Willie collected Booboo, who was curled up on the porch next to the woodpile, and with the dog waving his tail like a baton beside him, Willie whistled his way home.

He felt wonderful. It had been such a lucky day. He couldn't believe all the good things that had happened. First the compliment Jackson had given him, then the softball game with Milton, and now Marla was acting as if she might be his friend after all.

12

Being Responsible

*T*he doghouse already had a pitched roof by the time Willie got home with Booboo. Dad was standing front and center in the lighted garage beside it. "Where were you?" he asked Willie.

"Helping my friend. You weren't here when I got home, Dad."

His father grunted and gestured with his hammer. "So what do you think?"

"About the doghouse? It's neat." Willie looked at Booboo for his opinion, but Booboo was busy scratching his ear with his hind leg.

"Cutting out the door with a keyhole saw was pretty tricky. You might have learned something if you'd been here."

"Yeah, you did a good job, Dad."

Dad nodded. "Well, tomorrow you can help me do

the insulation. I have to buy a staple gun to tack it down. We'll get to it right after school, okay?"

"Okay. . . . You think we'll get done in time for me to go over to help my friend with her woodpile again?"

Dad frowned. "Her? Who is this friend?"

"She's a new girl in my class. Her family moved into an old house that they heat with a wood stove. It's a lot of work."

"They shouldn't be heating their house that way," Dad said. "Burning wood pollutes the environment. Adds to the greenhouse effect."

"But, Dad, they need to save money. Marla's mother's sick a lot, and her father doesn't have a very good job."

Dad grunted. "Is she the one you wanted to lend your tape player to?"

Willie nodded reluctantly.

"Best not to get mixed up with people like that, Willie."

"People like what, Dad? Marla's a nice girl. She can't help it that she's got problems."

"That's true, but people like her tend to take advantage of you, and you have enough problems of your own to handle right now, don't you?"

"Marla's smart, Dad." Willie figured if she wanted to be in school she must be smart. "And her mother's a teacher."

"Your friend Jackson's bright, too, isn't he?" Dad

asked. He put his hand on Willie's shoulder and squeezed it gently. "You're better off playing with him."

How did Dad know that when he'd never met Marla, Willie asked himself. The thing with Dad was he didn't trust people who were poor. He suspected they didn't work hard enough or weren't intelligent enough to get themselves out of their situations. He wasn't being fair, Willie thought. . . . And Dad wasn't always right either.

"Willie," Dad said, "why do you think I'm putting so much effort into this doghouse?"

"I don't know, Dad. So you can keep Booboo away from your paper?"

"No. So that *you* can train your dog. I'm doing it for you, Willie. And when I tell you things you don't like to hear, that's for your benefit, too. Do you understand?"

"Yes, Dad."

Booboo had been waiting patiently at the door to the house. Now he barked to be let in. Willie opened the door. "There you go, Booboo," he said, but all the whistle had gone out of him.

They had lamb chops, which were Dad's favorite, for dinner. Willie wondered what Marla was eating. Was she so poor she didn't get enough to eat? She didn't bring her lunch to school, and she didn't buy either. Tomorrow, he'd make two peanut butter and jelly sandwiches and give Marla one. He'd bring the tape player to class for her, too, because it was his, and he had a right to do what he wanted with his own things even if Dad didn't think so.

"How's the doghouse coming?" Mom asked as she served them the apple cobbler she'd made.

"It's coming," Dad said. "Tomorrow Willie's going to help me with the insulation."

"Good," Mom said. She smiled at Willie.

He smiled back, even though another afternoon of holding and standing wasn't what he'd call good. If Dad wanted to teach him how to work with his hands, why didn't he let Willie practice using the tools himself?

After dinner, Dad went to listen to the seven o'clock news. Willie cleared the table, and Mom put the dishes in the dishwasher.

"Well, I spoke to his secretary," she confided. "Ettie said his boss is going crazy without him. And there's a brand-new boiler on order for the customer, so that's no problem anymore. But Ettie says the boss is too proud and stubborn to call Dad to come back. It would be like admitting he was wrong."

"Dad's vacation time can't last forever, can it?" Willie asked.

"Just about forever. He gets six weeks, and since he's never taken what was due him any year before this—" Mom shrugged.

"So if Dad and his boss want the same thing, you

just need to get them talking to each other, Mom," Willie said.

"Umm. . . . Maybe I should tell him his boss wants to talk to him about how many vacation days he plans to take. Ettie would say she called *me* if I asked her to. Willie, you're a genius." Mom gave him one of her power hugs.

Willie ambled into the living room and was settling down to watch TV when Dad asked, "Did you finish your homework?"

"Oh, yeah," Willie said, as the two math work sheets and the map of the New England states he had to do popped into his head. "I better do that first, right, Dad?"

"Right," Dad said with an approving nod.

First Willie put the tape player in his book bag before he sat down at his desk so that he wouldn't forget it. Dad would probably get angry if he found out Willie had lent it, but for once Willie didn't care.

• • •

Big snowflakes were falling thick and fast, speckling the air outside Willie's bedroom window the next morning.

"Dad, if we get enough snow for sledding, could I go for a while after school and then do the insulation?" Willie asked impulsively at breakfast.

"Work first, play later's the rule my father taught me," Dad said.

"Yeah, Dad," Willie said. The trouble with the rule was, there wouldn't be any daylight left for sledding after the insulation was done.

At his school bus stop, Willie watched the floating snowflakes transform themselves into a thick frosting over trees and lawns and rooftops. The first snowflakes of the season were so beautiful. They were sort of the flowers of winter, he thought.

The sledding would be great if this kept up, but Dad had said insulation first. Rats! Work and responsibility seemed to be all Dad understood. Had he ever done things just because they were fun when he was a kid?

Willie could remember a time, before he started school and life got complicated, when all he had to do was play. What a thrill it had been to skim downhill on his first plastic sled! He bet Dad couldn't remember a pure fun time like that. Was it because he was so old or because he'd never had fun? Poor Dad, Willie thought as the bus nosed around the corner.

13

The Extra Hour

*I*t was still four weeks to Christmas, but Mrs. Tealso already had Jackson and Nedra putting up Christmas decorations around the homeroom.

Willie lingered at the bulletin board to study the pictures of Christmas celebrations on display there. Next to a Swedish Christmas tree with lighted candles was a menorah with kids lighting Hanukkah candles. He wondered if Mrs. Tealso thought Hanukkah was like Christmas. It wasn't really; it was about a miracle that happened during a battle the Jews had fought back in biblical times.

Dad was half Jewish but he didn't practice any religion. Mom was Catholic. She prayed to the Virgin Mary when she was worried, and she went to mass at Christmas, but she wasn't very good about explaining what it all meant. They both said Willie could decide what he wanted to be when he grew up. Maybe he wouldn't be any religion either, Willie thought. He wondered what Marla was. Protestant probably. Most people he knew were Protestant—Jackson and Milton were, anyway. Would there be any difference between a Protestant Christmas tree and a Catholic one?

Most of the trees pictured on the bulletin board had piles of presents under them. Because of Mom, Willie's family had a tree every year and exchanged presents. *Presents*, Willie thought, and he almost groaned aloud. He'd meant to save up his allowance, but Dad had told him it was his responsibility to buy a new leash after Booboo chewed his old one to pieces. Also, at Thanksgiving the florist had a special, and Willie wanted to show Mom how special she was to him. She had been so thrilled by the mixed bouquet of fall flowers that he didn't regret buying it. Presents that weren't expected were really more fun. Except he was pretty broke now. He sat down to think with his elbows propped on his desk.

"What's the matter with you?" Jackson asked. He'd returned to his seat after hanging the last candy cane.

"I'm broke."

"You need some money? I could lend you fifty cents. I just got my allowance."

"No, thanks," Willie said. "I need enough for Christmas presents."

"Make them," Jackson suggested.

"I can't make anything," Willie said. He thought of the way he'd messed up when he tried to nail a wooden box together and had split all the wood. He could draw a picture, but Mom already had a whole wall of his pictures in the family room. "Nothing good enough, anyway."

• • •

By lunchtime the snow was a foot deep, and it was still falling. Milton and Patrick sat down with Willie and Jackson again, as if they were all friends now. Maybe they were, Willie thought. It surprised him that a kid could become his friend without him having any choice in the matter. Not that he minded, he was just surprised. Plus, it must mean Milton had decided he was an okay kid. Yes, it had to mean that because Milton would never make friends with a goofball. Willie sat up straight and looked at the three boys at his table from his new perspective. He was a regular guy now. He'd been chosen!

"I hope it snows all day and night," Milton said. "My dad's letting me borrow his snowblower this winter. I figure I can clean up fifty, sixty bucks after school doing driveways."

"You're lucky," Willie said. "My father'd never let me borrow his blower. He thinks I'll get my fingers or toes sliced off with it."

"You probably would," Milton said. "You gotta be strong to wrestle a snowblower around."

"I shovel my neighbor's walk for a dollar," Jackson said, "and she gives me three dollars to do her driveway."

"That's all you get for a whole driveway? Boy, are you getting rooked," Milton said.

"Well, she's old. It's like doing her a favor."

"I could shovel driveways," Willie said. "I bet I could." The idea excited him. *That's* how he could earn money.

"Finding customers's not that easy," Milton advised him. "Everybody's signed up with a plowing service already. And if they do hire you, they'll try to rook you because you're just a kid."

"You mean they don't pay?" Jackson asked.

"I mean—like one guy told me I didn't do a good enough job, so he was only giving me half. But I fixed him. I blew half the snow right back on his driveway."

"Was he mad?" Jackson asked.

"Sure, but so what?" Milton said.

"Milton don't let nobody mess with him," Patrick said.

Willie didn't think he could be that tough because he hated getting yelled at. But he shouldn't let people take advantage of him either. Dad said a man had to stand up for his own rights. He could *try* to be tough, Willie decided. He didn't know if he'd go so far as to shovel snow back on where he'd just shoveled it off, though.

Marla had come in late again. There she was sitting at the garbage pail table alone. Today she was reading. Willie took out his notebook and did a quick cartoon of her—all hair and a book. He took the cartoon and the peanut butter sandwich he'd made for her over to her table.

"Fun-ny!" she drawled when he stuck the cartoon under her nose.

"And this is for you," he said. "I made it myself."

She wrinkled her nose at the peanut butter and jelly sandwich. True, it had gotten squished out of shape in his book bag, but he'd put it in a plastic bag to keep it clean. "I don't really like peanut butter," she said, "but thanks anyway."

He took the sandwich back. "Want me to bring you some cookies tomorrow?"

"You don't have to bring me anything, Willie."

"But I want to."

That finally won him a meltdown of a smile from her. Suddenly he remembered what else he had for her and eagerly dug the tape player out of his book bag. "Here," he said, "so you can dance. But I can't come help you with the wood because I've got to help my dad with insulation."

She picked up the tape player and offered it back to Willie. "Thanks," she said, "but I—it's too cold to dance in the barn now."

"Please keep it. I want you to have it."

"I don't think my dad would let me. He doesn't like me to accept favors."

"Oh," Willie said. "So how's your mother?"

"The headache went away this morning." Marla's face brightened. "She said she might unpack some of the boxes if she feels well enough. Most of our stuff's still packed in them, and it's hard to find a place to do my homework with boxes all over the place."

"Well, you could come to my house," Willie said. "Or go to the library."

"If Mom stays well, maybe I could go to the library," Marla said.

Not his house, Willie thought regretfully, but the library. She still wasn't that eager to be his friend.

• • •

Everyone got excited in social studies when they heard school might close early because of the heavy snow. Willie was reading about farming in New England, but his eyes kept shifting to the window. A miniature snowdrift had grown mouse deep on the sill outside. He longed to poke his finger into the pure, perfect stuff, but for that he'd have to get up and open the window. Their social studies teacher, Mr. Grey, was a good guy. Good enough to let Willie get away with it? Willie stood up. "I'm just going to open the window," he said.

"No, you're not," Mr. Grey said. "Sit, Willie."

Willie sank back into his seat.

Classes were about to be dismissed at the regular time when something interesting happened. The principal announced over the intercom that the buses were running an hour late and everyone should return to their homerooms to wait. Instantly, a long line of kids calling home for a ride formed at the phones in the hall near the office. Willie looked out the picture window at the big hill behind the playing field and had a brainstorm.

"Let's go sledding," he said to Jackson, who was standing next to him in a cluster of their classmates. Marla was there, too.

"With what? We don't have our sleds," Jackson said.

"It's junk pickup day," Willie said. He pointed to the garbage pails, overflowing with sticks and furnace filters and paint cans, in front of the houses facing the school. Parts of furniture stood alongside the pails at the curb. "Come on, Jackson."

Willie grabbed Marla's hand. "You come, too," he said. "We're going sledding."

She looked at the hill with longing. "I used to have a sled," she said.

"So come on," Willie urged. "Let's see what we can find." The three of them raced out of school, crossed the street, and began picking over the discarded junk.

Willie found a plastic potty seat. He grinned and tucked it under his arm. Jackson shouted gleefully when he came up with an inner tube that even had air in it. Marla seemed reluctant to touch anything. She just stood around looking. Willie spied a plastic laundry basket with one broken end. Marla could just fit in that. He dumped out the roofing tiles the basket held and took it.

"Let's go," he called. "We got what we need." Jackson caught up with him halfway to the hill. Willie turned and found Marla at his heels.

Jackson got to the top of the hill first and went sailing down on his inner tube. The tube flattened a snow path that would be easy to follow.

"Here," Willie said to Marla, "you use the basket."

"You're not going down on *that* thing," Marla said. "It's a baby's toilet seat."

"It'll work," Willie assured her.

"It's too small. You'll kill yourself."

"No, I won't. Watch me."

He sat down on the potty seat and pushed off, facing backward with his feet in the air and his arms stretched wide for balance. "Yahzoo!" he screamed as he rode the river of snow down, down to the sound of Marla's high laughter, until oops, he hit a bump and tumbled into a snowdrift.

"Willie!" Marla screamed.

He struggled up and out of the drift, raising his

arms overhead and yelling again, "Yahzoo!" to prove he hadn't been hurt. Then he went digging through the snow for his potty seat.

He found it and looked up to see Marla kneeling in the basket and sliding sedately downhill. She was gripping the sides and grinning so broadly her tongue and teeth showed. At the bottom she rolled over deliberately, and then rolled again in the snow, so that like him, she came out powdered in white from head to toe.

"You look like abominable snowmen," Jackson said.

"Who're you calling ab*dom*inal?" Willie asked and leapt at Jackson, knocking him down and rolling him in the snow until he, too, was powdered.

Marla shrieked with laughter. She tried to make a snowball to throw at them, but the snow was too dry to stick in a ball.

"Let's go down again," she suggested. This time she led the way up the hill.

"Let's go down together," Willie said, "and see who's the fastest."

He fell off the potty seat midway down the hill, and Jackson's tube won the race. Each of them took a turn on the tube. Nobody wanted to try the potty seat. But Jackson went down in the laundry basket, and Willie made himself into a rolling pin and rolled down the hill, gripping his arms and legs tight against his body. They were having such a good time that they would have missed their buses when they finally came if Jackson hadn't spotted his.

"There's bus 54. I'll see you guys tomorrow," he yelled out. He left the inner tube at the foot of the hill and sprinted for the bus. Marla ran after him.

Willie dumped the potty chair in the basket and dragged it and the inner tube back to the curb where they'd found their snow vehicles. Littering was high up on Dad's list of unacceptable behavior, especially public littering. "You should leave a place clean for the next person who uses it," Dad often said. It was one rule that made sense to Willie.

He hoped Dad would understand about his playing first instead of working. After all, it had just happened that way by accident, thanks to the snow.

14

Willie's Report Card

*F*riday was a bad-news day. First Mrs. Tealso announced report cards were ready and everybody would return to homeroom for the last ten minutes of the day to receive theirs. Lots of kids groaned. Willie's stomach flip-flopped like a fish out of water. His marks might be as bad as last time. They could even be worse. Unless he'd done good work that he wasn't remembering. Or unless his teachers had gotten the Christmas spirit early. "Let's give the kid a break, and throw him a few Bs for a change," Mr. Grey could have said. Willie toyed with that pleasant possibility. No. Mrs. Tealso would have said what Dad always did, that you should earn what you got in life.

Jackson bent down and pretended to search for something that had fallen on the floor near Willie's desk. "Willie," Jackson whispered, "it's supposed to snow some more today. You wanna shovel driveways tomorrow in your neighborhood?"

Willie bent his head down, too, as if he were helping Jackson look.

"Yeah. I'll start scouting for customers tonight," Willie said.

"Okay. I'll bring my shovel first thing after breakfast."

"What are you two looking for?" Mrs. Tealso wanted to know.

"Found it, Mrs. Tealso," Jackson said. He held up his pen as proof.

Since homeroom had officially begun, the best way to reach Marla on the other side of the room was by note. Willie wrote one asking her when she was going to meet him at the barn. At the bottom of the note, he drew a really neat spider in a web. Then he folded the sheet up small, addressed it, and passed it to the kid next to him. Milton was sitting along the postal route. The note got to him just as Mrs. Tealso stepped out of the room to talk to the teacher across the hall. Willie couldn't believe it when he saw Milton unfolding the note.

"Hey, Marla," Milton said loud enough to get the whole class's attention. "Willie wants to know if you'll meet him in the barn. Will ya, huh?"

Boys hooted as if the question meant something dirty. When Willie saw Marla cringing in her seat, he went berserk. He hurdled a desk and jumped Milton to grab the note away from him, but Milton turned and hunched over so that Willie found himself hoisted onto Milton's back with his feet off the ground. Just then Mrs. Tealso returned. She caught Willie clinging to Milton as if he were stuck midway in a leapfrog game.

"Willie Feldman! *What* has gotten into you? Step outside in the hall and stay there until I finish taking attendance."

Out in the hall, Willie leaned against the door, which Mrs. Tealso had firmly shut behind him. Some friend Milton was turning out to be! Boy, would Willie be in trouble if Dad heard about this. The instant Mrs. Tealso gave him a chance, before she could decide it was all his fault, Willie had better spit out a convincing explanation.

"I'm innocent, Mrs. Tealso. Milton took something that was mine and he—" No, the trouble with that approach was she'd want to know what Milton had taken. Mrs. Tealso didn't allow note passing, not even in homeroom. She took homeroom seriously. She said they had to pay attention so they'd know what to do in case of an earthquake or if their bus schedule changed. All right, then, how could he defend himself?

"Milton was teasing me, and I was trying to make him stop."

"By jumping on his back?" Mrs. Tealso would ask next. Then she'd send Willie to the office for fighting.

Willie was still leaning against the door, trying to come up with a good opening line, when the door suddenly gave way. Unable to stop himself, he went hopping sideways across the front of the classroom as far as Mrs. Tealso's desk with his arms outstretched for balance and one leg up in the air. She stood gaping at him from the door, still gripping the doorknob. Meanwhile the class was falling out of their seats laughing. Willie hadn't meant to be funny, but since he obviously had been, he took a bow.

The bell rang.

"Way to go, Willie," someone said and slapped him on the shoulder as the class rushed past Mrs. Tealso to get to science on time.

Even Marla was smiling as she left. That was his only comfort, that he had made her smile again.

"Willie," Mrs. Tealso said. "*What* am I going to do with you? If I didn't already have to see your parents because of your report card, I'd have to call them in about this. You get more outrageous every day."

"But—" Willie said.

"No excuses." Mrs. Tealso raised her hand in a stop sign. "Just go to your next class and try to behave yourself the rest of the day."

Willie slunk out of the room. Never mind his tussle with Milton, Mrs. Tealso was seeing his parents about his report card, which meant it was really bad. His only defense for now was not to think about it until he had to. But everywhere he turned kids were whispering, "Report card, report card." So much anxiety in the air made it hard to breathe.

The end of the day came far too quickly and there it was in his hand—a report card that spelled disaster in Ds and Cs.

"Well," Mrs. Tealso said to him quietly as he stood beside her desk to receive it, "this is not a report card your parents are going to appreciate, is it, Willie?"

He shook his head, too crushed to answer.

"It's too bad you only came after school that one time to catch up."

"Yeah," Willie said, recalling how magically easy she had made problem solving seem that afternoon. "I guess I need help bad, Mrs. Tealso. Could I stay after from now on? I mean, I'd really appreciate it if you'd let me."

Mrs. Tealso brightened considerably. "How about if I give you some extra time during your recesses instead?"

"Okay," Willie agreed. Unflinchingly, he would cut recesses out of his life forever. He even managed to say, "Thanks, Mrs. Tealso."

He was so worried about his report card that he forgot the question in his note to Marla, but she didn't. She whispered to him before he got on his bus. "Sunday afternoon around two, in the barn. Okay?"

"Huh? Yeah, sure. Okay," Willie said.

It was snowing again, not just a flurry but a steady fall that was whiting out everything in sight.

"See you tomorrow, Willie," Jackson said.

"Yeah, if I'm still alive after my father sees my report card."

Jackson gave him a sympathetic shove and wished him luck. Willie watched Marla climb into her bus alone and sit down alone. Was he her only friend? He hoped she wasn't counting on his company Sunday, because Dad might just ground him forever.

The report card could disappear in a snowbank, of course, but Mrs. Tealso was calling his parents, so that wouldn't solve anything. On the other hand, why rush into the jaws of punishment by handing it over immediately? The thing to do was give Mom a preview of the bad news and let her ease his way to Dad.

• • •

If Willie hadn't known the man working on the doghouse in the garage must be his father, he might not have recognized him. Dad's nose was red from the cold, and he was wearing a grease-streaked red-and-black-checked lumberman's jacket and a red flannel hat with floppy earflaps. He looked a lot more dignified in a business suit and tie, Willie thought.

Yesterday Willie had held shiny strips of foil-covered insulation while Dad banged them into place with a staple gun. Today it looked like it was going to be plywood boards.

"We're almost finished, Willie," Dad said in cheerful greeting. "Soon as we get these boards nailed on, your dog can move in. It's too cold to paint the house until spring. Think he'll like it?"

"I don't know, Dad," Willie said cautiously. "It's not heated."

"*Heated?*" Dad said indignantly. "Don't be ridiculous. What do you expect for the mutt, hot and cold running water?"

"Maybe we could run a heating pad from the house to the yard," Willie suggested helpfully.

Dad snorted. "Hold this for me," he said.

And Willie held.

Dad kept measuring and readjusting and planing off edges. By the time Dad had driven in the last nail to complete the giant doghouse, Willie's hands, nose, and toes were stinging with cold, but with his report card in his pocket, he didn't dare complain.

"Now let's see if we can carry this to the backyard," Dad said.

The doghouse weighed a ton. They staggered to the backyard with it and dumped it right under Willie's bedroom window.

"It's too close to the house here," Dad said.

Willie thought fast. "Well, but, Dad, if Booboo gets lonely and cries in the night, I can lean out my window and comfort him."

Dad grunted in weary agreement.

Mom had dinner ready when they finally got inside the warm house, but she looked distracted and Booboo wasn't anywhere in sight. Mom waited until Dad had gone to wash up in the bathroom before telling Willie what she was upset about.

"Your father's right about Booboo, Willie. That dog does need to be trained better," she said. "I had to lock him in the basement again. I didn't tell your father why. I just said he pestered the women at my Hospitality Club meeting here this afternoon, but that's not why I'm punishing him."

"What'd he do now?" Willie gritted his teeth in anticipation.

"He jumped up on my bed where the women had left their coats and chewed the fur collar off Mrs. Law's jacket. I told her I'd take it to our tailor and have a new collar put on. But, Willie, you know what that will cost? And I don't know where I'll get the money."

"Don't tell Dad, Mom, please. I'll pay you back, whatever it is. Just don't tell Dad. He really will send Booboo to the pound."

"Don't worry," Mom said. "I'll find the money somehow."

Dinner was eaten in silence. Usually Mom would chat about something, but she was brooding, and Dad seemed too tired even to comment on the day's quota of bad world news. Willie hardly knew what he was eating. He was busy figuring how how to present his report card.

After Dad retired to the living room to watch the

six o'clock news broadcast, Willie took a deep breath and said, "Mom, I got my report card."

She raised one eyebrow at him. "Good or bad?"

"The worst." He handed it to her.

For a long time she stared at the report card, making a "tsut, tsut, tsut" sound. Next she began slapping the card against the back of her hand and chewing on her lower lip as she thought.

"No good hiding it from Dad," Willie said, reading her mind. "Mrs. Tealso's calling you both in for a conference."

Mom groaned. "You're sunk, then. This is coming in too hard on the heels of everything else."

"I know." Willie gulped. If Mom was giving up, then it really was hopeless.

After the news broadcast ended, Dad took one look at the report card and squeezed his eyes shut in pain. While Willie and Mom held their breath and stared at him, Dad sat in his armchair with his eyes closed and the report card in his hand. Finally he looked at them and said, "Well, we can't afford to start Willie in a private academy until I get my job situation straightened out, but as soon as I do, we better send him to learn some decent study habits."

"Don't send me to another school, Dad," Willie begged. "I like the one I'm in now. I'm going to stay in recesses with Mrs. T. from now on and catch up."

"Whose idea was that?" Dad asked.

"Mine," Willie said.

His father nodded without expression. "And your teacher's willing to use her free time for you that way?" he asked.

"Yeah. She's a really good teacher, Dad. She's like you. She takes her job seriously."

"It's about time *you* began taking things seriously," Dad said.

"I'm going to try," Willie assured him. "I'm sorry I keep messing up. I'm really sorry."

Again Dad nodded. "Good," he said, finally. "Good."

•　•　•

Bedtime came and with it the hour of Booboo's banishment. Mom tied an old wool scarf around Booboo's neck. She kissed his nose and said she forgave him for chewing up Mrs. Law's collar. Willie snapped on Booboo's leash. Booboo wagged his tail happily, and off they went.

When they got to the doghouse, Willie tried a positive approach. "See, Booboo, Dad built this just for you. Pretty neat, huh?"

Booboo looked at Willie hopefully, then began pulling toward the gate. He obviously thought he was going to get an extra walk. To get him into the doghouse, Willie had to crouch and shove. Once in, Booboo turned around and barked at Willie as if asking what the joke was. Willie unsnapped the leash. "Stay,

Booboo." He backed away. Booboo promptly followed him to the gate. Willie slipped through it and locked it behind him. "It'll be warmer in the doghouse. You might as well go back in."

Booboo looked doubtful.

Mom leaned out Willie's bedroom window to ask, "How does he like it?"

"Do you have an old blanket or something for him, Mom?"

"Wait there." She disappeared and came back with the tattered comforter that Willie had clung to until just last year.

"You saved it!" Willie was touched.

"I couldn't bear to throw it away. You loved it so," Mom said.

Willie bundled the comforter into the doghouse in a pillowy heap. "There, that'll keep you warm," he told Booboo and shoved him back into the house. This time Booboo seemed to get the idea. He lay down. Willie ducked back through the gate and locked it behind him.

The whining had started by the time Willie finished his shower and climbed into bed. Soon afterward, the whine became a bark. For an hour Booboo barked. Dad yelled out a window, "QUIET, BOOBOO! QUIET!"

More barking. More commands from Dad. Next Dad appeared in Willie's bedroom. "Are you asleep yet?"

With Booboo barking in his ear how could he be? "No, Dad."

"Then talk to your dog. Tell him if he doesn't shut up, we'll send him back to the pound tomorrow."

That's how it would be, Willie thought with a sinking heart. The dog pound for Booboo and a private school for him. Banishment for both of them. Unless he could think of a way out.

15

The Tough Customer

Sleep was a bumpy road for Willie that night.
In between dozing and leaning out the window to
plead with Booboo to be quiet, Willie was kept awake
by his dog's howls, yowls, whines, whimpers, barks,
yips, and moans. Booboo's range of loud noises was
impressive.

At midnight Dad stormed into Willie's bedroom.
"We're getting phone calls from the neighbors. Go
get Booboo. Lock him in the basement."

"But you won't take him to the pound, will you?"

His father grimaced. "One more chance to adjust
to the doghouse is all that dog's going to get. Tomorrow night is it."

"Thanks, Dad," Willie said. "You're a good guy."

Dad grunted. "He's got to learn, and so do you,"
he warned before leaving Willie's room.

Booboo was tail-wagging, tongue-licking happy to

be rescued—until Willie locked him in the basement. Then Booboo restarted his song of complaint. At least, from the basement, it sounded muffled.

In the morning, right on schedule, Jackson and his snow shovel appeared on Willie's doorstep.

His struggles with Booboo had made Willie forget that Jackson was coming. "I didn't have a chance to get any customers yet," Willie said. He yawned, so tired from his sleepless night that all he wanted was to go back to bed.

"We can get them together," Jackson said. "You ready to go?"

Willie yawned again. "Sort of." He went to tell his mother where he was going.

She was in the kitchen with Dad, who was drinking his morning mug of coffee. "Why don't you come Christmas shopping with me, Harold," Mom was saying. "Then you can monitor what I spend."

"No, thanks. Just don't buy everything in sight because it's Christmas and I gave you back your charge plates. Remember, I may still end up out of work for a while."

"Well, but didn't your boss ask you when you're coming back?" she asked. "And he took care of the boiler problem the way you wanted, didn't he? What more do you want from him?"

"I want him to trust my judgment from now on."

"Oh, Harold! You want him to say you were right, don't you?"

Dad sniffed as if he'd been caught out. "Wouldn't you say he owes me that much?"

"He has his pride, too," Mom said.

In the silence that followed, Willie mentioned his shoveling venture. To his amazement, they both approved. Dad even suggested a price, ten dollars for a driveway and two dollars for a walk, unless one or the other was longer than normal. Willie got the snow shovel from the garage while Jackson came into the kitchen and made polite conversation with his parents.

"Were your parents happy with your report card?" Dad was asking Jackson when Willie got back with the shovel.

"Yeah. I got an A in math. Last quarter I got a B. My dad gave me a dollar."

"Good for you," Dad said. "An A is worth a dollar in my book."

"How about fifty cents for Cs?" Willie suggested hopefully. He had Cs in social studies and science, Mr. Grey's courses.

"Fine, minus a dollar for every D. That would leave you owing me how much, Willie?"

"See you later," Willie said and pushed Jackson out the door.

Willie considered taking Booboo along, but Booboo would only get in the way. Better leave him in the basement to sleep off his exhaustion from last night's concert.

There were twenty-two houses on Willie's lawn-proud street, and until he and Jackson circled back to the twenty-second house, they got no business. Most people's driveways had already been done. In a few houses no one answered the bell. Some homeowners said they were planning to snow blow their own driveways. Three said they'd hired someone who hadn't come yet. At the twenty-second house, which was right next door to Willie's, the elderly widow, Mrs. Lima, answered the door. Yes, she would hire them to do both the walk and the driveway, she said, and she nodded at the price when Jackson mentioned it.

"She's not poor, is she?" Jackson asked uneasily after Mrs. Lima went back inside.

"I don't think so. Her husband owned the department store in the mall. She's pretty crabby, though. We better do a good job."

They did a fine job, getting every bit of snow off right to the edges of the walk and driveway. When they finished they rang the doorbell, sweaty but pleased with themselves.

Casually Mrs. Lima glanced at the driveway and sighted along the walk. "Just a minute," she said. She dipped back inside her house.

"Maybe she'll give us a tip," Jackson said. "Twelve dollars isn't much for the ton of snow we shoveled."

"I don't know," Willie said doubtfully. "She had a

big fight with my mom for cutting some roses off a bush that was growing over the fence into our yard. Mom says Mrs. Lima's stingy."

How stingy they found out when Mrs. Lima returned and handed them each a five-dollar bill.

"It was ten for the driveway and two for the walk, that's twelve," Jackson said. "You owe us two more."

"I never said I'd pay you for cleaning my walk."

"Yes, you did," Jackson said.

"I certainly did not, and ten is all you'll get from me." Mrs. Lima shut the door. Period. End of discussion.

Willie rang the bell. The door whipped open. "You better be on your way, young man, or I'll call your parents and tell them you're harassing me," she said. Before he could get a word out, she shut the door again.

Jackson scowled. He stood there with his arms folded and his big brown eyes glaring. "Know what we should do, Willie? We should do what Milton did; put the snow back."

Willie groaned. "I didn't get much sleep last night."

"Come on, Willie. We can't let that mean old lady get away with cheating us."

Willie took a deep breath. "Okay," he said. "Okay."

It didn't take long, mostly because before they'd

shoveled half the snow back on the walk, the door flew open and Mrs. Lima demanded to know what they were doing.

"You didn't want us to do your walk, so we're putting it back the way it was," Jackson said.

"Fresh-mouth kid!" the woman snapped. "What's your last name?"

"You can call my father," Jackson said. "He's a policeman and he doesn't like people who cheat."

The door slammed hard. Mrs. Lima was stronger than she looked. A minute later it opened again and there she was with two dollars in her hand. "Now I want you to shovel the walk," she said.

"The price has gone up a dollar," Jackson said.

Willie gulped. Mrs. Lima didn't say a word. She paid the extra dollar and shut the door. When they'd cleaned off the walk for the second time, they left. Willie waved at the window from which she was watching them, but she didn't wave back.

"Think she's going to call our parents?" Jackson asked.

"I don't know. Probably she'll call mine," Willie said. "My dad's already mad at me and Booboo." He could feel the tangled knot of worry growing in his chest.

"But we didn't do anything wrong to that lady."

"Maybe not, but she's an adult."

"Yeah, I see what you mean," Jackson said.

Willie invited him to come in to play, but Jackson

said he'd better get home. He gave Willie the extra dollar and told him he could pay the fifty cents when he had the change. "Or you can keep it," Jackson said. "I mean, you're the one's in trouble."

"Thanks, Jackson," Willie said gratefully. He and Jackson gave each other a high five.

The phone was already ringing when Willie walked into the house. "Yes," he heard his father's voice answering in the kitchen.

Willie pulled off his jacket and boots in the hall. He had no doubt it was Mrs. Lima calling to complain.

The money he'd earned was in his jacket pocket. What would six dollars and fifty cents buy? Not a tape deck for Marla. Maybe a Christmas flower arrangement special for Mom. But she loved roses. He'd buy her one long-stemmed rose and get Dad a cactus plant. Something with prickers that you better not touch should suit him.

The phone call must have ended because Willie could hear both his parents yelling at each other in the living room. He heard his name. It made him feel guilty to have them fighting about him, even though he hadn't done anything wrong this time. He guessed he'd better try to defend himself. Taking a deep breath, he stepped into the living room.

16

In the Doghouse

*H*is parents were at it so hot and heavy they didn't even notice Willie standing there. Usually, Mom gave as much as she got from Dad, but today she seemed to be losing ground. Dad's voice had a bad-weather sound to it.

"I told you you were spoiling that boy," Dad was saying, "and now you see how right I am? He goes from one idiotic escapade to another. He's got no sense. Him and that ridiculous dog you let him pick."

"Willie is a good, sensitive, wonderful boy," Mom protested. "You just don't appreciate him because he's not like you."

"Then I suppose you think his report card is fine?"

"No, I didn't say that."

"And phone calls about how he hoodwinked a

poor widow out of her money—that's just fine?" Dad asked.

"She's not a poor widow. Mrs. Lima's a not-very-nice *rich* lady, Harold. Ask Willie for his side of the story, why don't you."

"I intend to, but first I want *you* to understand. You always take his side. That's part of the problem. You won't discipline him. You stick me with that job. No wonder my son thinks I'm mean."

"He doesn't think you're mean, Harold. He loves you."

"Dad," Willie said. And then louder, "DAD!"

"What?" Both parents turned to look at him.

"Dad, I'm sorry about the report card and all that, but I didn't do anything bad to Mrs. Lima. She told Jackson and me to do the walk and the driveway, but then she wouldn't pay us for the walk, even though we did a good job. So we just put the snow back. That's all."

"According to Mrs. Lima," Dad said, "she never told you to do the walk because she doesn't use it. She goes through her garage. And you wouldn't take her word for it. That's what upset her the most, that you acted as if she meant to cheat you."

"But she did, Dad."

"Willie—" Dad hesitated. Then he shook his head and said, "I don't know who to believe."

"Me. I'm your son, and I don't lie. Much," Willie

amended carefully to cover any white lies he might have told.

"That's true," Mom said. "You know that's true, Harold."

Dad lifted his bony shoulders and let them drop. "All right. It's possible Mrs. Lima's getting forgetful and thinks she told you just the driveway. In any case, I want to satisfy her, especially after we kept her up last night with the dog barking. So you just return the money for the walk and say you're sorry. Say you must have misunderstood her."

"That's not fair," Willie said.

"Fair or not, it's foolish to make bad feelings with a neighbor over three dollars."

"But Dad—" Willie couldn't find the words for it, but he knew there was a flaw in his father's reasoning. Wasn't Dad holding out for an admission from his boss that he'd been wrong?

"Here." Dad took three dollars out of his own wallet and handed it to Willie. "Go. Just give her this money and say you didn't mean to upset her. . . . Put on your shoes and your jacket first."

Willie looked at Mom, who shrugged her shoulders.

It wasn't fair, Willie thought resentfully as he marched down his driveway and up Mrs. Lima's with Dad's three dollars pinched between his thumb and index finger.

Mrs. Lima answered her door, dressed in a wool suit with a lot of gold chains. "Here's your three dollars back," Willie said. And he added, "I'm sorry my dog kept you awake last night."

"You can keep the three dollars," she said stiffly. "I just wanted to teach you a little respect for your elders, Willie."

He nodded. "Okay." He turned to leave.

"Willie," she called. "You can do my driveway and walk again next time it snows."

"No, thank you, Mrs. Lima," he called back politely.

Her eyes went wide with surprise. Then she shut her door fast.

She might have won, but that didn't mean he was ever going to let her trick him again, Willie told himself. He went back home and returned Dad's three dollars to him.

"So, you and Mrs. Lima made friends?"

"No," Willie said. "But I did what you told me."

• • •

Booboo was still asleep on an old rag rug near the furnace when Willie opened the basement door to collect him for a walk. Leaving Booboo to sleep, Willie went to answer the phone, which had started to ring. It was Jackson. He wanted to know if Willie could go sledding in the park.

"Your snowboard's still in my car," was all Dad said when Willie asked if he could go.

"I know, Dad. I can double up on Jackson's sled."

"Listen, Willie," Dad said. "Do you really mean to knuckle down and work to bring up your grades this time?"

"I'm going to try, Dad."

"Okay. You might as well use your board. Who knows how much snow we'll get this winter." Dad went to the garage for the board.

Willie got tears in his eyes. He couldn't believe Dad was really going to give him back his board when he still hadn't become the son Dad wanted him to be. "Thanks, Dad. Gee, thanks," he said when Dad returned with the board.

"Just be careful with it, and wear your helmet," Dad growled.

In the park, Willie and Jackson slid down the hill along with a couple of dozen kids whose turquoise and red and pink parkas shone like neon lights against the snow.

Milton was there on his snowboard. "Wanna try mine?" Milton asked Willie when they happened to be climbing the hill side by side. "It's faster than yours."

Willie hesitated, remembering how Milton had gotten him in trouble by reading the note to Marla aloud. But you couldn't expect a friend to be perfect, Willie decided. "Sure, thanks," he said.

The snow was packed down hard and slick, except for the ridges made by sleds with runners. It was cold, but not cold enough to burn cheeks and noses—a perfect sledding day, Willie thought happily as he walked home from the park in the late afternoon.

He wondered what Marla had been doing. Having fun, too, he hoped. Tomorrow, he'd meet her at the barn. The ditches between the barn and the road might be frozen, and they could go sliding on them. Maybe he'd bring her a present like cookies, or candy, or something to make her laugh.

That night Willie put Booboo to bed in the doghouse and explained to him about Mrs. Lima and about Dad and the dog pound. "You be good, Booboo. This is our last chance," Willie said. Then he gave Booboo his best sneaker to chew on, tucked the old quilt around him, and asked, "Understand?"

Booboo tilted his head one way and then the other, all bright-eyed innocence. Like a battery-operated toy with a new battery, he was set to go. Well, Booboo should be full of energy. He'd slept half the day in the basement.

Willie went up to his bedroom and waited. Fifteen quiet minutes later, he began to relax. He was considering going downstairs to watch TV when the whining began. A few barks followed. Willie stuck his head out the window and warned Booboo to be quiet, but getting his master's attention just made Booboo bark louder.

At Mom's suggestion, Willie took some doggy treats out to Booboo. Then at Dad's suggestion, he went outside and smacked Booboo's rear end with a newspaper. "You be quiet," Willie commanded. Finally he yelled at Booboo, loud as he could, to STOP THAT. Since he didn't know what else to try, Willie got ready for bed.

By the time Willie was out of the shower and into his pajamas, Booboo was howling pretty steadily and the phone was ringing.

A minute later Dad came upstairs looking grim. "Go bring that dog inside. Put him in the basement. Tomorrow he goes to the pound."

"Wait, Dad," Willie begged. "I've got an idea."

"It better be a good one. I want that animal silenced, and if the only way to do it—well, you know I don't make threats I'm not willing to carry out."

"I know, Dad."

His father nodded wearily. "I'm going to bed myself now," he said.

It was still early. Dad must be really tired, Willie thought. He got dressed again and put on his winter jacket. He even took gloves and a hat before sneaking out of the house.

At first it was pretty warm in the doghouse with Booboo. What with the comforter under him and Booboo curled up contentedly against his stomach, Willie was well insulated. Soon he was yawning. He'd had a tiring day, and he still hadn't caught up on last night's sleep. Wrapping his arms around Booboo, he dozed off.

He woke up shivering. If an ice cube could feel, this is what it would feel, Willie thought. Eskimos must be pretty tough to sleep in igloos, unless igloos were warmer. Maybe Dad should have built Booboo an igloo instead of a doghouse. But Booboo didn't seem cold. He was jerking his foot, running in a dream. Willie tried to ease himself out of the doghouse without waking him. It didn't work. No sooner did Willie get his head far enough out to see the moon shining like a big, white ornament in the bare branches of the tree above him than Booboo's head butted his. The dog was ready to play.

It had to be the middle of the night, judging by how silent and dark everything was. Booboo had better not start barking now. Willie crept out of the doghouse and tried the door to the kitchen. It was still unlocked. Dad always tried the doors before he went to bed. Lucky he had gone to bed before Willie had retired to the doghouse.

As quietly as possible, with Booboo's toenails clicking on the stairs behind him, Willie returned to his bedroom. Even under all his covers with his dog snuggled close, he had a hard time getting warm enough to fall asleep again. Rubbing his chin against Booboo's springy fur, Willie made a promise to himself. No way was he going to let Dad return Booboo to the pound. No way was he going to let anything happen to his dog.

17

Hiding Booboo

"**W**illie, what are you doing in bed with Booboo?" Mom's anxious whisper woke him instantly. "Are you crazy? Your father will *kill* you."

"I got cold," Willie said.

"What?"

"Booboo wouldn't shut up, so I camped out in the doghouse with him, but I got cold in the middle of the night, so I snuck up to bed."

Booboo wriggled out from under the covers and pushed Mom's hand with his nose. She petted him absently, but her mind was still on Willie. "My poor angel! You really slept in the doghouse?"

"It was okay, Mom. I wore my winter jacket and gloves and a hat."

His mother wasn't consoled. Her eyes smoldered as she muttered more to herself than to Willie, "I can't believe he'd be so mean. Except he might make himself do it just to prove he doesn't go back on his word." She inhaled deeply. "I'll talk to him." Abruptly she kissed Willie and slip-slapped from the room in her velvet scuffs.

Having Mom fired up and on his side was a comfort, but Willie wished he could win one for himself, this one in particular because Booboo was his. What if—what if he hid Booboo somewhere?

Click, came the idea for the perfect place, far enough away so that Booboo couldn't be heard, and yet not so far he couldn't be fed. Willie rolled out of bed, glad to find himself still dressed and glad it was Sunday so he didn't have to go to school. He used the bathroom, then put on his winter jacket and lugged Booboo downstairs. Booboo enjoyed being carried. He dangled his paws comfortably and licked Willie's chin.

Outside the kitchen window, the dawn of a winter morning had tinted the sky a bright pink. Luckily neither Mom nor Dad was downstairs yet. Food, Willie thought. Booboo needed food and water in the barn, and something warm to sleep on. One of Mom's huge shopping bags was big enough to hold Booboo's dishes, a bag of dog meal, and the floor cushion Booboo used for TV viewing. But where were they going to get water? Unless Marla would help with that.

Booboo was too deliriously happy on the hike to the barn to mind the bitter cold. He ran loops around

Willie, stopping to investigate a ditch, starting up a bird, almost getting hit by the lone car coming down the county road as they crossed it. Willie didn't warm up until they reached Marla's house.

Only a few logs were left on the woodpile on Marla's porch. When he went to ask for water, Willie would carry some wood for her from the huge pile in back. But he'd wait a while. It wouldn't be polite to knock on her door before breakfast.

He set Booboo's cushion next to a post in the barn, out of the way of any drafts. Booboo settled down on it immediately and began licking the bottom of his chilled paws. "I hope you like it here," Willie said. "Anyway, it's better than a doghouse."

Booboo stopped licking and looked up at Willie expectantly.

"And you can bark all you want," Willie said. "Dad won't hear you, and neither will Mrs. Lima." Willie gave Booboo a hug and threw a stick, which Booboo just glanced at; the walk had been exercise enough for him. When Willie retrieved the stick and dropped it under his nose, Booboo did rouse himself enough to pin the stick with a paw and begin chewing it.

It was time to go carry wood for Marla.

On his third round with the wood, Willie heard a dog barking in the distance. Booboo? Probably, but the noise wasn't loud enough to bother Marla's family inside their house. He was still stacking wood on the porch when the door opened and a slight, balding young man with Marla's dark, expressive eyes asked him, "What are you doing?"

"I'm a friend of Marla's. I'm helping her," Willie explained.

"Well, that's really nice, but you're disturbing my wife."

Willie must have looked confused because the man explained, "When you put the wood down, she hears the thunk and it hurts her head."

"Oh, sorry." Willie backed off a step.

"You're Willie?" the man asked. Willie nodded. "I'm Marla's father. I've heard about you," Mr. Carter said. "Marla says you're the nicest boy she ever met. I'm glad I got to meet you." He smiled and held out his hand. Willie shook it. "Well, she'll be finished with her work soon if you want to wait. I'd invite you in, but my wife is—"

"I know," Willie said. "That's okay. Would you tell Marla I'll meet her by the barn, please?"

"Will do. Thanks for bringing in the wood, Willie." Mr. Carter waved in a friendly way and shut the door.

As soon as Willie returned to the barn and sat down on the floor cushion, Booboo stopped barking and began licking his face.

"You know what Marla said about me?" Willie asked him. "She said I'm the nicest boy she ever met. I guess she must like me now, huh? . . . But Booboo, you've got to be quieter or you'll wind up back in the pound." Willie didn't like to scare Booboo by mentioning it, but he knew that the pound waited only a few days for a dog to be claimed before putting it to sleep.

Booboo yawned. Willie yawned, too. He thought about taking a nap while they waited for Marla.

Next thing he knew, Booboo's tail was fanning his face and Marla was sitting there with her arms wrapped around her knees, watching him. "You sure can sleep anywhere," she said. "It's freezing in here."

"I was tired. See, I slept in Booboo's doghouse with him last night."

"You're kidding! You really slept in a dog-house? . . . You *are* a nut cake, Willie."

He wanted to ask her if that was better than a goofball, but for once he didn't feel like joking. He was too worried.

"What's wrong?" she asked after studying his expression. "Is it your father?"

Willie told her what Dad might do. ". . . So I'm hiding Booboo here," he said. "Could you visit him sometimes and bring him water?"

"Sure. I ought to be able to get out here once a day, anyway."

"Would you? That'd be great, Marla."

Her offer of help cheered him up until she added, "So long as I'm still here."

"What do you mean? Where are you going?"

She shrugged. "Nowhere if I can help it, but my father's boss changed his hours. Now Dad thinks the guy is taking advantage of him, and that's all it takes for my father to start thinking about where to find a better job."

"But you just got here. He's not going to move that fast, is he?"

She shrugged again, sad faced. "He might."

"But would your mother let him?"

"She hates the house. It's really the worst we've ever stayed in, and she's sure it's why she has the headaches again. I said we could just look for another place around here, but Mom's started talking again about how nice it would be if we moved back to her hometown in Texas."

"Texas?" Willie's heart sank.

"Don't worry. Dad will never go there. He says Texas is the last place in the world he'd try. He thinks it's full of phony cowboys and blowhards."

"What's a blowhard?"

"I don't know." Marla considered. "Someone who boasts, I think."

"I thought your mother was feeling better," Willie said.

"She was. She started putting the house in order, and she even said she'd look for a teaching job if she continued feeling this good. But then this morning while she was making us pancakes for breakfast, Dad told her not to bother looking for a job here because he's not happy with his. Just like that—" Marla snapped her fingers. "Mom's headache came back."

"I'm sorry."

"Me, too. I told him if he didn't like his boss, to find another job around here because I'm not moving. I'm *not*!" There were tears in Marla's eyes, and her lip trembled.

"Maybe he will find another job here," Willie said. "I mean, it could happen."

"Not likely. Dad's a sweetie most of the time, but he can be so stubborn you wouldn't believe it, and he's touchy."

"My dad doesn't change his mind easy, either. And he's proud."

"Do you hate him, Willie?"

"My dad?" Willie considered. "No. I get mad at him sometimes, but mostly I feel sorry that he got a goofup like me for a son."

Marla's eyes glistened with sympathy. "My father calls me selfish because I don't like staying home to take care of Mom, and he yells when he gets mad at me."

"Yeah, my father yells at me a lot," Willie said.

"But Mom calls me her angel girl." Marla smiled.

"My mom calls me stuff like that, too," Willie said. He crossed his eyes and hung his arms out, elbows up. "Look, I'm an angel."

Marla laughed. "Me, too." She imitated his pose. Then she said, "You know what I like about you, Willie?"

"What?"

"You're always happy, no matter what, even when things are bad for you. I wish I could be like you."

"You want to be a goofup? Now who's nuts?" he asked.

Her laughter tickled him. "How about we go slide on the ice," he suggested.

"Where?" Marla asked.

"At the bottom of the field. The ditches there'll be frozen now."

"Okay. I'll go back and tell them where I'm going, and I'll get Booboo a jug of water. Wait for me," she called as she ran out of the barn.

18

Dancing on Ice

Willie didn't have long to wait. Marla returned in a few minutes, breathless and rosy cheeked, with a plastic jug of water. Willie filled Booboo's bowl with it.

"Mom said to be back in an hour. She gave me her watch to wear." Marla held up her wrist. It was only nine thirty.

"Booboo can go sliding with us," Willie said. He covered the container of water with musty straw to keep it from freezing, and they set off.

The lower end of the field was a smooth pond of ice except where it was cracked and bumpy around the edges or where hillocks of dirt and grass stuck up. Willie took a running start and skidded sideways in wild abandon all the way across. Marla came onto the ice timidly, with small sliding steps. Booboo stood at the edge and barked. "Aren't you scared you'll fall, Willie?" Marla asked.

"No," he said. "If I crack my head open, so what? There's nothing inside it."

"That's not funny, Willie. And it's not true, either. You'd be smart if you paid attention."

"What do you mean? I pay attention."

"No. I watched you. You're always looking out the window or drawing or fooling around."

"Well," Willie said, "school's too slow. I get bored waiting." He was going to pay attention, though, he told himself. He was going to try and keep trying until he got himself trained. No sense making any promises. He'd just do it, starting tomorrow, Monday, when school began again.

"Come on, Marla. I'll swing you around." He picked up a tree branch thick as his wrist and twice the length of his arms. "Take one end and just hang on and lean back."

"Whee!" she squealed like a little kid as he swung her in a wide circle on the ice. She was plump, but so light he could have swung her forever while the sun glinted off her flying hair, but before long she asked him to stop. She rested a minute, then she started to dance on the ice as if she were a skater—except most of her movement was in the arms.

Willie watched and applauded. Then for a while they broke pieces of ice off the edges and sailed them across the slick center. Booboo chased after a chunk, and when his legs slid out from under him, he yipped in dismay. They laughed at his comical expression before he regained his footing and trotted back to them.

They discovered a spot of clear ice where they could look through to the grasses and moving water below. "I think I see a fish," Willie said. "Look there. Oh, wow, what a big guy. It must be a trout. Long as my arm. Too bad it got away."

"You liar," she said. "You didn't see any fish."

"Sure I did. What do you see?"

"You," she said and shoved him. "Just you acting up."

Water dripping over the edge of an undercut rock had made icicles. Willie broke one off and offered it to Marla with a bow. "Something to refresh you, modom."

She took the icicle and sucked on it. "Delicious," she said, imitating his fancy tone. "Have one for yourself, do."

"See that house way up there on the hill?" Willie said as he reached for an icicle. "I explored it once. Jackson was with me, but he wouldn't go in. I got in through the basement, and was it ever dark and scary! Want to go there with me sometime?"

"Not especially. What's inside?"

"Nothing. It's just one room with a wood stove, but you could make a fire in it to keep warm."

"If you had wood."

"There's wood there. All you need's matches."

She looked at the little house. It was set so deeply into the hillside that the underbrush would hide it in the summer. But now it stood out like a brown wart amid the skeleton trees on the snowy hill. "Maybe sometime I'll go with you," she said, ". . . if I'm still here."

"Let's slide some more," Willie suggested to wipe away her sadness.

They were holding hands and slide-skating on the ice with Booboo at their heels when Marla suddenly said, "Oops, it's over an hour. I've got to go."

"Like Cinderella," he said.

"So? Aren't you the frog prince?"

"Oh, yeah," he said, remembering the puppet. "Anyway, we had fun, didn't we?"

For answer she gave him a smile that warmed him from the inside out. "Come in and say hi to my mother," Marla said. "She liked you."

"I can't. If I don't get home, Dad'll send the sheriff after me," Willie said.

So few cars had passed along the snow-covered road that their footprints were still visible as they walked back to the barn.

"Willie," she said. "I don't really think you're a goofball anymore. I think you can do anything you want to do."

"Thanks, Marla," he said.

She left him at the barn and ran off to her house.

He watched her go, hoping she wouldn't move away. He'd never liked any girl as much as he liked her.

The minute Booboo was shut up in the barn, he started barking, even though Willie had promised he'd be back soon. It made Willie feel bad to hear that barking as he walked away. The barn was as cold as the doghouse. Booboo was going to hate it there alone in the dark.

•   •   •

Dad put down his newspaper when Willie walked into the living room. "What did you do with your dog, Willie?"

"I put him where he won't bother you."

"What? What do you mean?" Dad frowned. "Where did you put him?"

"I can't tell you that."

"What do you mean, you can't tell me? I'm your father."

"You said you were going to take him back to the pound."

"Oh, so that's it," Dad said huffily. "Well, just remember that your dog wouldn't be in trouble if you'd trained him. This isn't my fault, it's yours." Dad glared at Willie.

Willie blinked. He knew it *was* his fault in a way. He had been kind of lazy about making Booboo behave. And he *had* promised Dad before he got Booboo that he'd train his own dog. "Dad, you said you were going to take him to obedience school," Willie said. "Maybe I could go with you and learn how to train him."

Dad twitched his lip. "I'll think about it," he said. "Meanwhile, where did you hide him?"

"You're not going to take him to the pound?"

"I said I'd think about it."

"Well, but, Dad, I can't tell you unless you promise."

"You mean you don't trust me?"

"I trust you if you promise."

Dad's lips thinned. "YOU GET TO YOUR ROOM!" he yelled. "And think about this, Willie— the only bargaining chip you can use with me is doing better in school. When I see you improving there, then you can talk to me about your dog."

Willie clomped slowly upstairs. He had almost gotten another chance for Booboo, but somehow he had messed up on the negotiations. That figured. He'd never yet come out ahead in negotiations with Dad.

19

Both Gone

Willie meant to get up early Monday morning and go check on Booboo in the barn before school, but he overslept and had only enough time to make the school bus. Marla wasn't in homeroom. That seemed pretty normal. He just hoped her mother wasn't feeling too bad.

Mrs. Tealso had a rotating system for calling kids to do math problems on the chalkboard. Today Willie got called. It was a multiplication problem, and by some miracle he got it right. Without cracking a smile, Mrs. Tealso raised her hands and applauded him. The class did a double take and then applauded, too. Willie was so tickled he responded with a wolf whistle.

"Enough of that now," Mrs. Tealso said. "Everybody finish your work."

While his class filed out after language arts, Willie

hung back. "Sorry about the wolf whistle, Mrs. Tealso," he said when they were alone. "I got carried away."

"I know, Willie," Mrs. Tealso said. "Will I see you during recess as usual?"

"You sure will, Mrs. T. I'm gonna get a B in math this marking period, or anyway a C. . . . Maybe a C + ?"

"That's the boy, Willie!" Mrs. Tealso said. It was funny how kind her smile made her look.

• • •

Mom was dancing to one of her aerobics tapes when he walked into the kitchen after school. Before he could say a word, she grabbed him and made him swivel around the floor with her.

"Guess what, Willie," she said as they danced. "Your father's going back to work. He said he decided he'd made his point and it would be rubbing his boss's face in it to expect an apology from him. He's starting back tomorrow. Isn't that great?"

"Great," Willie said. "He listened to what you said, didn't he?"

"Oh, he listens to me. It just takes him a while to hear." She stopped dancing and turned serious. "Willie, your father's upset that you're defying him."

"You mean because I won't tell him where Boo-boo is?"

"What else?"

"I'll tell him when he says he won't send Booboo back to the pound."

Mom sighed. "You can't hide Booboo forever."

"I know that. Want me to tell *you* where he is, Mom?"

"No! It's better if I don't know."

"Okay," Willie said. "Then I can't tell you where I'm going now."

"Take some doggy treats along, and give him one from me," Mom said. Willie gave her a hug and took off.

It was dark by the time he got to Marla's road. The light in the windows of her house and the smoke coming out of her chimney were welcoming, but Willie was too anxious to get to Booboo to stop. He hurried on to the barn, which looked deserted in the chill winter evening.

"Booboo," Willie called. "Hey, Booboo, it's me."

The barn door was standing ajar. Willie pushed it all the way open and stepped inside. It was hard to see much besides shadows in the blackness, but he could feel the emptiness. Booboo was gone. Nothing was left in the barn, not the candles and matches Marla had kept on the windowsill, not even the spiders that had rebuilt their webs.

In a panic, Willie ran back to Marla's house and banged on the door. He stopped his fist in midair as he remembered how sensitive Marla's mother was to noise. Just then the door was flung open and there stood Marla's father.

"Marla—" Mr. Carter began eagerly, but his expression turned to dismay as he said, "Oh, it's you, Willie. Do you know where she is?"

"Uh-uh," Willie said. "Did Marla bring my dog here?"

"Not that I know of. She's gone." Mr. Carter rubbed one hand over his bare head. "I don't know anything about your dog."

"But where did Marla go?" Willie asked.

Her father stood aside. "Come in. It's cold out."

It was hot in the house, where the door to the wood stove stood open, revealing a nest of crimson coals. There were still some unpacked boxes in a corner, but the room looked much more homey, with colorful throws and pillows and lamps.

"Marla?" her mother called hopefully.

"Not yet, dear. It's her friend, Willie," Mr. Carter said. To Willie he murmured, "She's been frantic ever since Marla ran off."

"But why did she go? Did something happen?"

Mr. Carter nodded and confessed, "I told her we were leaving for Texas as soon as we get repacked, and she flipped out on me. Wouldn't even give me a chance to explain." Earnestly, he told Willie, "I'm doing this for my wife. Tyler, Texas, is where her family lives. They'll help if—it'll be good for Marla, too. She'll have cousins and plenty of adult relatives around. It'll give her a chance to be a kid again. Lately she's had too much responsibility on her shoulders, I know, but—"

Mr. Carter rubbed his scalp wearily. "Anyway, I no sooner said we were moving than she took off. Do you have any idea where she could be?"

Willie thought of the barn. He bet she'd gone there first. Where else would she go? School. But it was too far, and at night she couldn't even get in. Had she taken Booboo with her wherever she went? She might have so that she wouldn't be lonely. Suddenly he remembered telling her about the little house tucked into the hill when they were skating. She hadn't wanted to explore it then, but if she were desperate, and if the barn was too easy because her father could find her there, she might try the house.

"Mr. Carter," Willie said, "there's one place I know, but it could be a wild-goose chase. I better go check it out."

"I'll come with you."

"Okay, but if she's there and she sees you're with me—why don't you let me talk to her? Maybe I can convince her about the move being a good one."

Mrs. Carter appeared in the bedroom doorway wrapped in the man's bathrobe again. Weakly, she leaned against the door frame and said, "Let him go alone, dear. She can't be far away, and she trusts Willie."

"All right," Mr. Carter said. "I'll give you an hour to find her, Willie. Tell me where you're heading, though."

Willie described the house tucked into the hillside.

"Are you sure you want to go there alone in the dark?"

"I'm sure," Willie said.

Mr. Carter patted him on the shoulder and went looking for a flashlight to carry while Mrs. Carter said, "Willie, tell her this will be the last move and it's the right one."

"I'll tell her," Willie promised.

"Tell her they grow roses in Tyler, that it's not all barbed wire and tumbleweed like her father thinks." She smiled Marla's magic smile and Willie smiled back. "Thank you, Willie," she said. "You're a dear."

It was a long walk past the barn and down the hill to the field where he and Marla had skated. Willie was glad for the moonlight, which kept him company, and glad he had the flashlight as well when he saw the peaked shadow of the house barely visible across the snow-covered hillside. The sweet tang of wood smoke in the air told him he had guessed right. She was there, or at least someone was. Eagerly, he ran through the field and up the hill to the boxy house whose windows were boarded up with sheets of wood and crossed slats.

"Marla!" Willie called.

A dog barked in reply. "Hey, Marla, it's me, Willie. Let me in."

Booboo's barking got more anxious, but the door didn't open. Willie tried the latch without any luck. Well, he knew another way to get in. He circled around to the back, where a pair of doors were set into a bank leading to a dirt cellar. That was how he had gotten into the house last time.

He lifted one of the heavy doors and, with the help of the flashlight, felt his way down the concrete steps into the black maw of the dirt-floored cellar. It was barely high enough for him to stand up in without cracking his head on the overhead beams. Still, he moved quickly in a crouch to his right. The ladder steps there led up to the main floor.

When he entered the main room upstairs, he saw a dark hump in front of an anemic fire in the fireplace. "Marla," he said just as a pair of paws hit him hard in the stomach. Booboo was wriggling glad to see his master and as noisy as ever.

"How come you wouldn't let me in, Marla?" Willie asked after he'd quieted Booboo down. That was when he realized she was sobbing. He touched her heaving shoulders. "Marla, it's all right. Come on. Listen to me. You're going to like this move. Really. Now listen." To the back of her head, he explained what her parents had told him to tell her. "Are you listening?" Willie asked her.

"Yes," she whimpered.

"Well, so it sounds good, doesn't it?"

"Dad always makes moves sound good."

"But you'll have *family* to help you take care of your mother so you won't have to stay home from school. That'll be good, won't it?"

"Maybe."

"Marla, he's the only father you've got. You have to trust him."

"Why?"

"Well—" Willie was thinking about Dad. "That's the thing about being a kid. We have to keep trusting them even when they mess up, because they're the adults and we need them."

"Who says?"

"Look around," he told her. "How long can you stay here alone?"

She looked, and even though she didn't say anything, he figured she had to know the answer. A few days was the most she could last because where was she going to find food or enough wood to keep the fire going?

"You know what I'll miss even if it does turn out to be nice in Texas?" she said finally.

"What?"

"You. I never had a friend as good as you, Willie. You make me laugh."

Embarrassed, he said, "Yeah, well, that's what a goofup is good for."

She stood up then, and in the dark before the smoky fire, she put her hands on his shoulders and kissed him. "There," she said. "Now you're not a goofup anymore. I've transformed you."

"Wow!" he said. "Wow!" He was so overwhelmed, he didn't even help her douse the fire or collect the bundle of things she'd brought with her. And when she'd finished and told him to come, he followed her back to her house like a robot while Booboo pranced beside him enjoying the adventure.

Willie was still in a daze, but when Mr. Carter insisted on driving him home he said, "You don't have to. I can walk."

"The ladies would never allow that. You get in the car, Willie."

"Bye, Willie. See you in school," Marla said.

"Yeah," he said. "See you. Bye, Mrs. Carter."

Booboo followed Willie into the car without waiting for an invitation. He settled on the seat with his paws on Willie's lap and promptly fell asleep. Willie stroked the dog's fur. It was so good to have Booboo back. But what would Dad do about him?

20

The Prince

*O*utside the car window, the moon looked like a glimmering mirror of ice in the star-speckled sky. Willie tried to imagine what it would feel like to be standing on it, looking back at the blue orb of earth. Lonely, he suspected.

Mr. Carter got into the driver's seat and said, "The word from your friend is I'm to report on you to your father, Willie."

"About what?" Willie couldn't remember anything he'd done wrong recently.

"Let's just hope your father's home. Marla said it was important I speak to him."

When they got to Willie's house, Mr. Carter followed him into the kitchen. He introduced himself to Dad, who stood up and shook his hand while Mom hugged and kissed Willie as if he'd been gone a year.

"My darling, my angel boy!" she kept crying. "We didn't know what happened to you."

"Mom, I'm fine. Nothing happened to me. It was Marla and Booboo who were in trouble."

Dad was standing straight backed with an embarrassed grin on his face, listening to Mr. Carter, who was saying, ". . . I just need to tell you what you probably already know. Your son is a real prince. My daughter says he's the kindest and most understanding kid she's ever met. You must be very proud of him."

"Yes," Dad said. "Yes, Willie's a good boy."

Willie blinked, hardly believing his ears.

"Well, I'd better get home to my girls," Mr. Carter said. "Willie—" He extended his hand and shook Willie's firmly. "Thanks for all you've done for us." Then he said good-bye to Mom, and Dad walked him to his car.

The instant Dad returned, Willie asked, "Dad, what are you going to do about Booboo?"

"Do?" Dad frowned at Booboo, who was sitting at the kitchen table as if he were waiting to be served. "Well, I suppose he can sleep in your bedroom tonight."

"About the pound," Willie said. "You said you were sending him to the pound."

"But you didn't mean it, did you, Harold?" Mom asked.

Dad thought for a while before he said, "I did mean it, but I certainly can't return Booboo to the pound now, can I?"

"You can't? You mean, you love him, too, Dad?" Willie asked.

"No, I do not love Booboo," Dad said. "That foolish I'm not. But it seems from what Mrs. Tealso tells me that you're putting forth some effort in school, and I wouldn't want to discourage you from that. Besides, what your mother says is true, Willie. You're not like me, but you're fine as you are . . . and I *am* proud of you."

With a nod meant to confirm what he'd just said, Dad turned on his heel and retreated to his newspaper in the living room.

"Didn't I tell you?" Mom said. "See, Willie? And you thought he didn't care."

Willie stood there with a grin stuck on his face and let his mother hug him.

• • •

Marla came to school the next day, but it was just to say good-bye.

"Why, Marla," Mrs. Tealso said, "I'm sorry to lose you."

"Me, too, Mrs. Tealso," Marla said. "I liked it here, and I—" Before she could finish she burst into tears and cried so hard that Mrs. Tealso had to send her to the girls' room to get control of herself.

Jackson said good-bye to Marla at lunchtime when she sat at Willie's table and ate her sandwich from home and an apple. Nobody else said good-bye to her, not even Willie. The best he could do was walk her to her bus.

"See you, Marla," he said when she got on. He knew if he said any more, he'd start bawling, too. He waved, though. He waved at the bus and waved until his bus driver tapped his horn impatiently to remind Willie to board. The minute he took his seat on the bus, Willie turned his face toward the window to hide how bad he felt. He didn't see a thing outside that window on the way home.

Nothing much changed after Marla left except that Willie seemed to have become Mrs. Tealso's favorite student. He was putting in a lot of time and effort trying to learn math and language arts. Having something complicated to think about kept him from missing Marla quite so much.

Two weeks had passed when Willie got home from school one day to find a letter postmarked Tyler, Texas. "Dear Willie," Marla wrote,

> *Dad was right. I love it here. I've got three girl cousins I go to school with. One's in my grade, and one's ahead of me and one be-*

hind. And my aunts are neat. They're so kind to Mama. Oh, and Dad got a job right away that he likes so far.

Anyway, what I want to tell you is how sorry I am. I mean, I wasn't nice when I first met you because I thought you were a goofball and you'd mess up my life. How was I to know you were really my frog prince?

Write me, Willie. I miss you a lot.

> *Your friend,*
> *Marla*

"Nice letter?" Mom asked.

"Yeah," Willie said. "She says I'm her frog prince."

"Of course you're a prince. Didn't I always tell you?" Mom asked.

Willie laughed. It didn't matter if she had; she was his mother, so he knew better than to believe her.

"I'm going to write and tell Marla how Booboo's doing," Willie said.

He'd tell her that since Booboo was back in Willie's bed at night he was quiet—most of the time. An Booboo hadn't wet on any more crossword puzzles, either. Of course, Dad hadn't left any on the floor now that he was back at work and happy being busy again, but still Booboo deserved some credit.

Instead of a signature at the end of the letter, he'd draw a picture of a frog with his own face and a crown. Yeah, that'd be good. He bet it would make Marla laugh, and even if he couldn't hear her, he'd like that.

About the Author

C.S. Adler taught middle school English for many years, and is now a full-time writer of middle-grade fiction. She has more than thirty published books to her credit, including *Daddy's Climbing Tree,* her most recent Clarion novel; *Tuna Fish Thanksgiving*; and *The Lump in the Middle.* Ms. Adler lives in Schenectady, New York, and Wellfleet, Massachusetts.

BUTLER PUBLIC LIBRARY
BUTLER, PENNSYLVANIA 16001

  J F ADL
Adler, C. S. (Carole S.).
Willie, the frog prince / C.
S. Adler.